PENGUIN BOOKS

D0752817

A Dutiful Daughter

Born in 1935, Thomas Keneally was educated in
Sydney. He trained for several years for the Catholic
priesthood but did not take Orders. He began writing
when a schoolteacher and his first novel, *A Place At
Whitton*, was published in 1964. Since then some
eighteen novels and a children's book have been
published.

Many of his novels have been highly acclaimed. He
has twice won the Miles Franklin Award for *Bring Larks
and Heroes* (1967) and *Three Cheers for the Paraclete* (1968),
and the Royal Society of Literature Award for *The
Chant of Jimmie Blacksmith* (1972) (also a successful film).
Schindler's Ark (*Schindler's List* in the U.S.A.) was
awarded the prestigious Booker Prize (1982), the *Los
Angeles Times* Fiction Prize (1983) and is soon to be an
important film. His major novel, *The Cut-Rate Kingdom*,
was published by Allen Lane in 1984.

In 1983 Thomas Keneally received the Order of
Australia for his service to literature. He is married
with two daughters and lives in Sydney.

Other fiction by Thomas Keneally

The Place at Whitton (1964)
The Fear (1965)
Bring Larks and Heroes (1967)
Halloran's Little Boat (1969)
The Survivor (1969)
Three Cheers for the Paraclete (1969)
The Chant of Jimmie Blacksmith (1972)
Blood-Red, Sister Rose (1974)
Gossip from the Forest (1975)
A Season in Purgatory (1976)
Victim of the Aurora (1978)
Passenger (1979)
The Confederates (1980)
The Cut-Rate Kingdom (1980)
Schindler's Ark (1982)

T·h·o·m·a·s K·e·n·e·a·l·l·y

A Dutiful Daughter

PENGUIN BOOKS

Penguin Books Australia Ltd,
487 Maroondah Highway, P.O. Box 257
Ringwood, Victoria, 3134, Australia
Penguin Books Ltd,
Harmondsworth, Middlesex, England
Penguin Books,
40 West 23rd Street, New York, N.Y. 10010, U.S.A.
Penguin Books (Canada) Ltd,
2801 John Street, Markham, Ontario, Canada
Penguin Books (N.Z.) Ltd,
182–190 Wairau Road, Auckland 10, New Zealand

First published in the United Kingdom and Australia by Angus & Robertson Ltd, 1971
First published in the United States of America by The Viking Press, 1971

First published by Penguin Books Australia, 1972
This edition published by Penguin Books Australia, 1984

Offset from The Viking Press hardback edition

Made and printed in Australia by
The Dominion Press–Hedges & Bell, Victoria

CIP

Keneally, Thomas, 1935–.
A dutiful daughter.

First published: Sydney: Angus &
Robertson, 1971.
ISBN 0 14 003391 2.

I. Title.

A823'.3

For John Abernethy

1

It had been a thunderous spring. On Saturday, thunder again rolled over the Glover farm. Perhaps, even with four hundred of its acres swamped, it was not yet convinced of the powers of water. At the peak of her thirty best and merely sodden acres, Barbara Glover, in her kitchen, was taken by a sudden fury at the crisp network voice that said, "Further thundery showers." She dropped the half-drawn syringe of antibiotic and ground the radio knob to *off*, as if the broadcaster were vulnerable at her hands. Rain, she could see, was falling on the rim of mountains down which her brother was coming home. Or was supposed to have come home—yesterday. Barbara breathed and drew herself up to quash her sick anger at his culpable nonarrival, the sick longing for his coming.

Then the syringe again.

To her right, the bottom of the half-door was closed, and

3

the top leaf ajar. She heard from beyond the door the fractious shufflings of her father, her mother's frequent groans. The groans were a matter of course; though not to disturb her, Barbara. It was the father who became readily anxious.

"Barbara!" the father roared. He sounded firm, and might as well have. There were areas in which Barbara's dominance was absolute, and made a roar as irrelevant as a whine.

The girl sighed and laid the syringe on the draining-board again. Looking west once more through the kitchen window, she could have been thought to be love-sick.

"Oh, please," the mother said distantly.

Barbara lifted the syringe. In the strangely luminous gloom of the kitchen, she thumbed the plunger and saw a spurt of molten fluid rise from the needle. But even though moving towards the half-door, she seemed very indefinite about the syringe—its purpose, her intentions. It could have been a loaded brush in the hand of a painter lacking a theme.

When her hand was already on the half-door bolt, she caught a sound, the shrill of a truck in low gear. So too would her parents have heard and be hearing, their perceptions and the truck-whine growing drily in the hollow pre-storm air. The mother groaned with the foretaste of it; her son's holidaying eyes and ears coming within range of her symptoms, her distended glands and viscous discharges.

No one in the house moved.

There came the eking noise of brakes, and a slammed door, and the rattle of their gate being visited.

Barbara Glover's mouth moved with a certain avidity. She looked exceptional in that any shape her slow sweet lips made was both hesitant and imperial. Her beauty, like the beat of the visiting motor, ached in the air.

She tiptoed back to the splashboard and put down, yet again, the syringe. She formed a soft word.

"Damian," she said.

2

You are Barbara's brother Damian, sweating by the gate, waiting while a girl called Helen turns her father's truck on the tiny road. You watch the mauve slime hiss beneath the tires while she must reverse and turn, reverse and turn, reverse and turn again before she is pointed townwards. You would like to distract the house's eye from her by straightaway opening the gate and jogging up to the door. But, having spent the night with Helen and suspecting yourself of loving her—or, better still, suspecting yourself of being unwise not to love and marry her—you feel you owe her a wave-off.

She is a gay, bustling girl, the sort of trim and unamazed girl you would expect to find as features editor of the campus paper, or politicking around the students' council, or (in despair of administrators) painting "Grey-Arsed Old Men Know Nothing of Revolt" outside the staff club. She has descended from activism to take interest in you, Damian, and to cherish you for the safer part of the night in the guestroom of her parents' house in town.

On account of the lateness of your homecoming, you feel apprehension like a rash at the back of your neck. You wonder too, watching her joyous manhandling of the truck, whether you want to be committed to this sweet little activist. You try to envisage a context in which she and Barbara could *fruitfully relate*. But the project defeats you.

As she leans close and tensed over the truck's steering, her bent smile forces one from you. She leaves you with an affectionate clenched fist.

She could have a sports car, like the soft rich girls of the campus. Instead, yesterday, the two of you begged rides all the way down from your tableland university. She gave a special sauce to your homecoming, but then you had reached the town and your delight died. Fifteen miles east, on a road behind the beaches, was your own home, a journey you would have to make alone. Nor was there anywhere to kiss the girl good-bye on the wide-open streets of that hateful town; where courthouse, Methodist Church, Masonic Temple, and Caledonian Hotel all aimed their blunt faces against ripeness and the ache of the young.

Her parents, new to the town and making an impact, were both away at the family hardware business. You kissed her under shelter of banana trees on the back patio of the new house—three generations newer than Barbara's farmhouse, yet even more odious. Both of you were neutralized by new brick, white wrought-iron chairs and glass-topped wrought-iron table; both sapped by the separate home-Christmases that lay between you and a new academic year. Suddenly Helen was listless, said she needed rest, muttered unmagical good-byes.

You had merely to find a truck that was going by the beach road. Two mineral trucks stood in the railway yard. They would pass by that narrow alcove of swamp on which the elder Glover, your father, had staked everything when you were a child. Now you sat in the shade to wait for the drivers to come back; but were forced to pace, fearing that, paid by the load, they might come soon, before your homecoming courage could coalesce. Pacing, you brought on a thirst and went for beer.

On your way to the Caledonian, a sick hunger, rooted in Helen but overshadowed by your sister, slowed you. Was it that you wanted Helen so much as you wanted to want her? On the campus she was thought especially vivid, a cosmos of feminine interest. Beside Barbara she seemed pleasant and formal: orthodoxy was her keynote. Her face, breasts, and limbs seemed as orthodoxly laid out as the pattern of her rebel evangelism.

Barbara is the illimitable one: to talk to her is to see brewed up before you a discreet atmosphere of endless surprise. Isn't that so? You were on edge at having to return to her and to the seasonal infatuation that recurred each vacation. Wanting now to delay, you might curse yourself tomorrow for delaying.

A service station summed up your malaise. SWING INTO THE SPACE AGE WITH OUR WONDER ADDITIVE, it sang in luminous yellow on a black base. A maxim printed over a prison gate you hadn't yet sinned enough to enter. One day Barbara might turn you over to some neat girl from the world of wonder additives, prestige upholstery, barbecue pits. You wouldn't save your vigour then. You'd already seen the jaunty Helen go stale in such a context.

The bar, this afternoon being Friday, was full of farmers; their brown maltreated hands, slung loosely on the bar and as if in payment for beer, panicked you. Though not quite the same as your father's hands, they evoked them. You lost all courage, then, to face your father until this morning at the earliest.

So, drinking more in neglect of finding transport and allowing time for Helen to rest, you began to feel less of a transient.

The afternoon jolted forward, and you turned towards the girl's place.

And the keenest welcome. Her face looked fresh from water; her eyes had cleared. As if for you rather than to mock her parents, she had put on a light little-girl dress that showed off her nearly edible knees.

"I thought you were going home," she said. "The filial Damian."

You wilfully set your eyes at lambent innocence. "I couldn't face up to them. Not so soon after leaving you."

The girl frowned with a more authentic innocence than yours. "I'm pleased you came back." She took your wrist. "Look, I'll get someone to go to the Student Power Congress in my place. . . ."

With a contrite shrug of your shoulders, you promised her scant return for such a sacrifice.

"I can get the car most days," she went on proposing. "We can surf on those beaches, do our holiday reading together."

Her neat jaws champed on those nougats of words: *surf, beach, holiday, reading.* It was a torment to see her eyes kindle at these futile possibilities: the sharing of lonely beaches, the naked swimming and making of love, the arguing and declaiming, the mouthing of verse and rebellion.

"Helen, it can't be arranged. If only it could. It wouldn't be fair to—you know—pretend the thing was possible."

Then Helen took your hand and led you into the living room. After sitting you in an easy chair, she herself crossed the room and briskly sat, ankles crossed beneath her, in a large petit-point lounge. She seemed to align the forces of the room against you, to invoke the twenty-five-year-old photograph of her father in Air Force uniform, the wedding picture of her elder brother, the large silky-veined buffet crammed with china, the carpet whose pile grew like clover, the television cabinet topped with its programme guide. She seemed to be ironically saying, In the name of all these expensive items from the best bazaars of this, our Nullarbor of the spirit, confess!

"Now," she told you—and could have been a house-proud young wife cutting a salesman down to size—"now what about this family of yours? Are you ashamed or something?"

"Shame doesn't come into it."

"Well, what? I've just been talking to an old schoolfriend of mine. Her family's been in this valley for eons. She tells me there used to be talk of your parents being cripples, but she hadn't heard anything of them for years and—to be frank —thought they were dead or perhaps gone away?"

"Oh, yes."

"Oh, yes!" she repeated, rejecting it as an answer.

But before she could make any further demands the telephone rang. She rose and backed to it, keeping you in sight. For a second it seemed sufficient for your future happiness that you should be bullied endlessly in the direction of sanity by those brusque, pretty eyes.

"Yes," she said into the telephone. "Oh, Barbara Glover. Damian's sister? Yes, that's right. Yes, the newsagent was right. I *am* just home."

You felt afraid with a fear far more immense than the tensions between these two competing women, than anything they could do at the moment to punish you. And you knew that it was Barbara who had injected the moment with this nauseous terror. Your blood tingled in your cheeks, and you felt halfway compelled to snatch the phone and beg to be taken home.

"No . . . well, I couldn't say," Helen was temporizing in her crisp way, "because there are so many undergraduates on the road. If he was depending on other people for his travel. . . . No, I'm sorry that I can't. . . . No, no trouble. Please let me know if . . . All right."

With a few stressed, portentous strides she came back to her lounge and, with her eyes never leaving you, furled herself into a corner. You pretended to stare at your boots.

"She's going to hunt around the pubs for you. Don't you think you could go and tell her you don't want to go home yet?"

You gave a shrug and a short, breathy giggle that accused her of being simple-minded. "Aren't you glad I fled to you?"

"Darling," she said for the first time, sounding unpractised, like a child playing Happy Families, "I'm very flattered. But these are your family."

"And you think a person is bound more to a poor family than he would be to a wealthy one? Like yours?"

"Oh," she told you, in proof of her naïveté, "poor families are less arrogant, surely. What they do for their children is a genuine sacrifice, not just a tax paid so that they can drop your name at service-club dinners and discussion groups. They get very angry with me, my parents, because my education hasn't made me a refinement of them. Them with a vocabulary and the ability to speak about Big Subjects without making a fool of myself, which they suspect they're doing half the time without knowing it. But your parents—"

Your harshest groan stopped her. "Don't talk to me about my parents, for sweet Christ's sake, Helen. My sister's the only important one. Because my parents and me—you know—we rate according to how we relate to Barbara. She's the only absolute in our household. You know—we only really *exist* in as far as we trust her."

"She sounded pleasant," Helen suggested.

"Pleasant? It's the size, the pure bulk of what she's done. For us, I mean. I'm the one who gets away for an education. I'm the Glovers' gift to the outside world. I'm already—you know— *under suspicion* in her inner world. She's the one that's bound to *them*. What's the time? Four o'clock? She'll have to head home before much longer. To attend to my mother." You went on, speaking of a sad thing you felt you could not prevent. "She'll be running around the pubs, looking for me. Drunks will call out 'What about it darling?' "

"You're full of guilt, aren't you?" she glibly suggested.

"The more I'm away from it," you said, "the less I can face it. You'll think I'm some sort of neurotic."

"Of course you are." She sounded pert. "That's why I love you."

You were depressed by such coy nonsense, because you wanted to treat her as more than a refuge, you were actually doing your best to fall in love with her, to break your reliance on Barbara. But, her knees sedulously locked beneath her, the girl went on looking as pitiably avid and bright as a long reading of women's magazines could make a person; the path to her womb seemed suddenly as predictably laid down, with as much bland inevitability, as an expressway approach.

She smiled. She was not a possessive woman, but her smile seemed possessive. This, you knew, was your own fault: you were a temptation to anyone's possessiveness—being so passive, a boy waiting on a summons, some unlikely summons. Whenever you looked in a mirror you saw a long, soft, kind mouth which, you feared, might have been made to give some final assent to the impossibility of life, joy, and sanity. Hamlet, prince of the Glovers.

So you began to distract Helen with vivid anecdote. "Let me tell you how we live out at Campbell's Reach," you said. "Spelt R-E-T-C-H."

You were eloquent about the house, the mange-coloured damp spots from floods, the ugly beading which you could scarcely imagine anyone having the heart to nail to the walls, the walls themselves sprung away from the joists, the rooms full of the smell of earth that had not dried out in centuries.

"There's a bloody tarantula, big as a plate, who comes out at night on the ceiling and hangs right over my bed. He's been doing it since about nineteen fifty-four."

"Every night?"

You contradicted all science with a flourish of the hand. "Listen, don't worry what some nice Englishman in the zoology department tells you about the lifespan of spiders. None of it applies to that bastard."

And although you spoke mockingly, you felt a genuine fury

against that punctual tarantula. "No, I tell you. If ever you felt warm or safe or full of hope—*if*, notice!—out would trundle this whopping piece of spidery livestock to hang above your face. Really, I think he was just being sarcastic most of the time. You know—like a teacher who knows he's frightened shit out of the class and now he can have his little jokes with them? I think he's saying, 'All right, boys, nymphs, shepherds, and archangels, all right! We'll teach Glover to sleep with his mouth shut and his thing between his legs.'"

Helen gave a dissatisfied chuckle, while you felt alive with rhetoric. "And besides the tarantula and the damp spots, there is that aggressive bouquet, two parts shit and one part creosote, that tells you where the outhouse is. Someone should pressure-pack that. For homesick cow-farmers in the city."

Without warning, you saw that she was angry. She said, "I don't care how much damp and creosote there is in your ancestry. But you owe it to me to trust me."

To show what she meant, she walked in front of you to a framed reproduction of stallions gambolling in heavy surf under the threat of a storm. It was, you could see, terrible enough. "I trusted you and showed you all this!" She struck the discreet walls with the pad of her fist. "You're not the only one with tarantulas in your roof."

"I think that's a fine painting," you told her. "No, listen, don't be superior, just because we're prejudiced and know what expressionism is. God, if I liked that painting, really liked it, I'd be a king. And I'd certainly pity the poor bloody me I am now. With reason."

She gave the reproduction a final push, out of spite. Its thundery sky danced with the reflections of the thundery afternoon in which you both stood, debating.

At last you held your palms out to submit. "You want to know about my parents?"

"That's right."

"I can't give you every detail."

"Why not?" She was jealous of her honour, her ability to love everything except the hearty affluence of her parents.

"Why not? Because you wouldn't believe it." In fact, you were disturbed by the extent to which you were about to mislead her. Now that she had become somehow electric again, and distanced from her parents' house, she was once more clearly a girl to marry. Wisdom, if nothing else, told you.

"I'll tell you a story," you said. "About nature and man. To a police magistrate, nature's what happens most of the time. You know. If you put a hundred male guinea-pigs in with one hundred female ones, and ninety-eight of the males importune ninety-eight of the females, well that's what a police magistrate would consider natural. No matter what the remaining four individualists happened to be up to."

"So endeth the first lesson," she mocked.

You took what seemed an angry handful of your own stomach flesh. "No, it's a subject close to my guts. If that makes them decadent guts, I'm sorry. Back to nature! There was a family out on Campbell's Reach, one of the better ones. Pious as hell. Prayed their arseholes off. They had a little boy. Hay-coloured hair. When he's four he gets sick and begins to change into a girl. When the change seems complete, he or she dies."

Helen frowned over the story, as if trying to stop herself from saying how much she hated stories like that. "The fact that he died indicated that the change was against his nature," she said.

"No. Maybe he just died because of the family's general demoralization. You know—at finding themselves treated so badly by something as reliable as their idea of nature."

"That's a dreadful thing to say about his parents," she couldn't prevent herself from saying.

"You see, we're all stuck with this idea of nature as being not only glossy and restful and honest and definite, but something outside of us. Bom-tiddy-bom-tiddy-bom-bom-tiddy-bom," he sang to a melody from the Pastoral Symphony. "In fact, nature doesn't exist except in our minds. Nature is a habit of our minds. There aren't rules, if people would only realize."

Helen herself was beginning to clock-watch. "Look, I think you've been sidetracked."

"Oh no," you told her, "the fact is not simply that Barbara is—you know—in a sense *enslaved* to them, because she feels outsiders will mock them. No, that's just half of it. The deeper truth is that they might only seem unnaturally—well—afflicted; they might only seem it because of a habit of our minds, and that if we had the courage to break that habit, even at the cost of going insane, we could be free people. The four of us."

"How would you break such a habit?" the girl asked, a little hushedly, in reverence of the risk involved.

"I don't think you would know that until the moment the chance came," you said, and then thought for ten seconds. "You hear of five-legged calves being born, with a third front leg growing stupidly out of their chests. Ah, big news! Farmers come from all over the river expecting to see the great believe-it-or-not sight. They see it. Then the owner splits the poor thing's skull with a mallet and buys himself a lottery ticket for luck and calls it *Tripod*."

"Don't make me sick," said the girl.

"My point is that if our habits of mind made it acceptable to people that—you know—twenty per cent of six-year-olds changed sex, we could accept it. We'd be prepared to say to people, 'How's your little boy transforming? Yes, I can remember how touchy Bert was while transforming to Bertha.'"

The girl laughed despite herself. "That's appalling," she said.

"But," you urged, "it's because of our habit of mind that what we call nature gets its fun, its dividends. Not only in terms of —you know—crucified flesh, but also because most of the moral blindness is derived from our poisonous"—you shook your head at the extent of the damage—"poisonous concept of what's *natural*. Our judgment words—abnormal, subnormal, deformed —*de-formed*, no less!"

Through the half-opened blinds behind Helen you could see

high-school boys biking home. They could be heard calling out to one another, because for them it was Friday, a bounteous afternoon, and *Gunsmoke* on the television at eight.

"Well," said the girl, her hands joined in what seemed piety, "I gather that your parents are handicapped in some way."

"They're dwarfs," you lied, putting a hand over your mouth and weeping gratefully into it. Helen jumped up to hold your jerking shoulders. Even through your shirt you could feel the coolness of her arm, and again decided it would be excellent for the future to have such cool arms to fall back into. Yet you knew that such decisions were not entirely your affair.

"Hairy little faces," you let yourself sob. "Christ, I don't want to have to see those hairy little faces."

Helen had made you coffee, over which you mooned, no more easy at misleading her, but committed now.

"You're free," she urged you, though she had begun to smoke in a clipped, urgent way, and took frequent squinting readings from her watch, all of which seemed to cast doubt on her own freedom at homecoming. "You're free to spend the night in town if you want. But you ought to tell your sister. Then she can go back to your parents knowing where you are."

"Yes," you agreed. "But she's had the trouble of being with them all the year, every solitary day. You can't expect her to be too tolerant if I can't—you know—*make myself* go home at the proper times."

"You'll have to have a difference of opinion over that."

"Her temperament doesn't allow for differences of opinion."

"Whose does?" She hissed smoke out between her teeth.

"Yes," you admitted softly. "But I'm not a coward, Helen. I *am* going back."

"Who says that's not cowardice?"

You shrugged. How could you tell her that it was more your sister's bountiful mystery than the family's impasse that brought you home three times a year? Your frightened hope was that she would no longer allure you. They were not two feuding hopes—the desire to find yourself both free of Barbara and slave to her. At their core they were the one wish. For she was a sign of contradiction, your dark avatar of a sister, and therefore had the power to make you lose at any of your homecomings.

"I make her sound a shrew, a proper bitch," you admitted. "In fact she's the quietest girl I've ever met. But she got her power at what was a dangerous age. Twelve. There she was— you know—*pubescent*. And taller overnight. Inches taller than my parents. I don't have to tell you how violently powerful a twelve-year-old girl can be. I don't blame her for any of it. She was incredibly fair. And my parents did become children in some senses, you know, transferring more and more authority to her. And not realizing that authority frightens her. Anyhow, power's bad for a twelve-year-old, and she certainly developed methods of dealing with debate."

"You're not making this up?" Helen asked.

"She was only a child and she had the responsibilities for imposing penalties. She must have been awfully lonely. The trouble is that a twelve-year-old can be terribly—sort of assertive. She still is, in a quiet way. Not so much assertive as— well, she's the focus of the house, as I was saying. The *house morality*—it's all in terms of her. I've broken it by staying here."

"Nonsense," said that carping, liberal, untested hostess of yours.

"Yes. Listen, you can't have parents like mine and lead a gay life on campus at the same time, unless there's someone there, at home, doing well by them, keeping them safe, out of trouble."

"Keeping them safe? Are they cooperative?"

"They suffer to some extent from . . . confinement."

"You don't mean locked up?"

"To some extent. Enough to guarantee they remain people in their own right."

"But they *are* people in their own right. Without being locked away."

You shook your head at finding her so solemn over habeas corpus. "My parents are of a certain type of person . . . about whom you could say that . . . in the absence of clearheadedness in the rest of the community, they're safer in jail. Nor are you exactly an average specimen of the type of people you find in this valley. They're bored and stupid, too dense to have a very active sort of malice. Out of pure vacancy they chain up their children—"

"Ah!" she mocked. "That makes for a change."

"They interbreed," you gave her as a climax. "And you know what a northern rivers farmer is at heart. *Gay insouciance*. Gay insouciance means they'll root a black gin just for experience, and if not a black gin, maybe a brood mare. And if not a brood mare—why not a midget?" For a crazy second you roared as men do at the height of bravado in pubs! "Hey, did I tell yer about the night Clarrie rooted the midget? Christ! Funny? I nearly shit myself."

There was a certain thrill from hearing Helen making affirmative noises through closed lips. The inference was that she herself had seen gay insouciance, its paradoxes.

"As long as you nearly shit yourself," you commented, "anything's permissible." You held a silence. "Anyhow, I think I'll always believe that, given her social background, Barbara's decision was amazing. Her ability to cope with it once she'd made it—that was pretty remarkable as well."

Watching Helen's eyebrows arch quickly once, you thought there was a momentary jealousy in her face, that she wanted to show up the folly of Barbara's primitive regimen.

"Yes," you went on, "she freed them by hiding them away. She made a world for them by letting them vanish from the world's memory."

"That sounds epigrammatical," the girl complained. "As if the two of you made it up as a salve for doubts. You must have doubts."

You denied it. You could have doubts only when there were two actions to choose between. . . .

But Helen raised the question of those memory cells of a bureaucracy reinforced with computers: electoral rolls, health-department files, taxation records. Even on a literal backwater such as Campbell's Reach you could scarcely fail to kindle a response in some department file, to spark the electronic curiosity of a departmental IBM.

For Helen's sake you started on a history of the Glovers, from the days when your father bought four hundred and thirty acres of marsh behind a particular superb beach. You were seven at that time, and the very number, four hundred and thirty, resounded in your head like a definite promise. The promise had to do with the beach being so good that it would become a resort. Then the swamp would be reclaimed. When the day came, you Glovers would become a rich family. The day never came—it might have; it did for many another swamp-bound farmer milking his cows by the light of a kerosene lamp.

That was the year in which Barbara took control. At the time you had envied her power. Now you were aware of how deep her terror must have been. Her terror in the night, with no one to call out to, because already she was the ultimate power against phantoms. You had her; she had no one.

It was after a night alarm that Barbara had taken power.

"Farm kids are supposed to know everything basic about physiology. It's presumed that they take note of the goats and cows and so on. But the part Barbara knew nothing about was that one night when she was twelve she would begin to bleed."

She had got up from her bed urgently enough to wake you. There was no electric light, and she fumbled at lighting a candle. When light sprang up, you could both stare—totally uninformed—at the ooze of blood on her nightdress. Before your eyes, she twitched when a new gush came.

She told you that she was dying. You thought so much of her in those days that you believed all her panic had risen because she could scarcely imagine how the three of you could survive without her.

You began to howl, while Barbara paced up and down in the hope that people didn't die in midstride.

No one came to help you. The candle burned out, and when it did, the dawn threatened greyly outside, cockerels could be heard, and three early hornbills creaked seaward over the house. Best of all, she announced, the blood on her dress had dried. Then she packed the caked fork of the garment over what she must have thought of as her wound, and you both went back to sleep; the last sleep of both your infancies.

"Why?" Helen asked, "Why do you say it was the last sleep of your infancy?"

"Because I pity myself," you said flippantly and neatly passed on to the tea parties.

Barbara held tea parties from the time of your parents' accident until you were about ten. That always made her seem very fallible to you: you weren't considered bona-fide dairy farmers, you weren't in the Cooperative (you added to your earnings by selling bait), and a large piggery north of the town bought your whole milk production. And Barbara was stung by your lack of status as a family. So she invited children to Saturday afternoon teas, to prove you had quality.

("People are so vulnerable," Helen muttered, intolerably pat.)

Your parents stayed in the barn, your father prohibited from smoking his aromatic mixture while visitors were with you. And visitors (girls from school, that is) patently envied Barbara, the way she was dominant in a house that had pots and crockery and a fuel stove. So, at the table, they would tend towards boasting, to being too talkative, too amply smiling. Then they turned home through the gate, their heads in a huddle, whispering like a nascent League of Decency. And Barbara would seem gratified.

"But surely the schoolteacher at Campbell's Reach. . . ?" Helen suggested.

"Oh yes, our guests told the teacher we had no parents, and he visited us as a duty. But our parents were in town, Barbara told him. And she could always bring a letter to school signed by my father. See, the teacher couldn't give a damn if Barbara was mistress in her own kitchen. All he wanted was not to have to write long letters to the Child Welfare."

Not that there had been many afternoon teas; Barbara soon worked her way through all the possible guests. There had been perhaps four such salons, but the last one had given them the status of an institution. Retrospectively, in your mind. A girl, a shallow fat girl, a genuine mudflats sow, was teased for her fatness by one of the other guests. She answered by repeating some half-rumour she'd heard about your parents. You, in your tight pants at table, watched Barbara, who seemed herself to remain passive, but from the jug in whose hand water, just off the boil, seemed to leap out at the fat girl. The skin on the girl's arms reddened and shrank, even in the second it took her to rise up and shriek. Her friends watched her convulse, then began to pull her party dress off her.

It was characteristic of Barbara, her seemingly passive way of inflicting torment, as if she herself were a primary victim of the hot water, as much as the fat girl. Which was not far from the truth, because the girl's mother, as big and vicious as you would expect her to be, called on your mother and, finding she wasn't (of course) in, beat Barbara up with a lump of red-box from the fireplace.

The startling aspect of Barbara's judgments was that she had never chosen wrongly when the question was either to admit or deny their existence. She kept them registered for voting, but did not let them cast postal votes. For this involved mail addressed to them. Willingly she paid the statutory fine levied on nonvoters. Yet, in the case of compulsory tuberculosis X-rays, she contrived to find half-castes to take the treatment for them. There were many reasons for the difference: the fine was higher for X-ray evasion; doctors as well as public servants were involved in correspondence between health department and the X-rayee. There was danger in that those who were willing to take an X-ray under another person's name had often startling pulmonary histories of their own. You had to find some healthy vagrant or fringe-dweller who needed the price of a drink. It seemed incredible to you, as you sat in Helen's lounge-room telling her of Barbara, that periodically your cautiously strenuous sister managed to recruit such people.

In the same way, she never pretended that they were dead or gone away. She and your father between them devised a perfectly legal document giving ownership of the farm to Barbara, in trust to an uncle who lived in another state.

Throughout the recital, the image recurred of a tall girl, more concisely boned than yourself, wearing eyes that have a convent privacy about them, and a secret, firm mouth. Standing on the street side of this or that bar, she parts the fug of tobacco smoke and country obscenity and squints a little, to spy out you, her big-boned, edible brother.

You must have seemed so pitiable then that Helen rose and approached you, taking your head against her stomach. Your arms hung inert against her hips. How guilty you felt for doubting that you loved her. But did a person lie to someone he loved? Did he take two uninterested handfuls of her hips?

You muttered, "They'll both be dressed in their best and full of excitement. I should have gone. They'd know already I'm not coming. But secretly, not saying anything to each other. They'll get tired—it happens in an instant. They wake at dawn, you see, and there's a point in the afternoon, you know, a certain angle of the sun, when they simply turn themselves off. It isn't such a bad life they live."

Once again you could feel tears on both cheeks. What bathos!

"It's a matter of their battening onto you, picking over your experiences. My mother's the worst—she doesn't even think in real terms. They suck on a person's experience. Barbara's good with them. She can convey experience very . . . atmospherically. She saves them every detail of her Friday trips to town.

Town being this town. The big cultural watershed, God help us!"

They had red wine at table to honour Helen and yourself, but it was easy to feel unwelcome, for the goodwill so signified seemed brittle and token. It took four glasses to convince you that you were not making a convenience of Helen. And a fifth to make you secretly formulate plans for Helen. Her father was pleasant, harried by success, her mother ferociously pleasant. Her throat was coired in pearls, and she wore her breasts like a brunt, no haven for men or babies. You would save Helen from her, free her to become something more than her mother's negative.

You were forced to tend this way by your over-all policy: to fall in love before you saw Barbara again.

"There's a clean towel for you, Damian," said Helen's mother, with a standard hostess smile. You could sense the resistance in her—you do not dress well, and she worried about leaving you to a room which had been made sacred by Helen's successful brother. Belching politely, you sat on the bed. To your left was an intimidatingly large map of the United States with what might have been isohyets marked in red, yellow, green, blue, pink, and violet wool. To your front, on pegboard, were a series of reproductions labelled "Impressionist," "Expressionist," "Fauvist," "Dadaist," "Cubist."

Obviously a boy who didn't want to be caught after dark in a country town not knowing his Dadaists from his Fauvists, you muttered in mockery; in fact you were made conscious of your alien slovenry by such thoroughness, and by the chronologies and valency tables that were pegged above and below the paintings.

You turned the light out as soon as you could. But the moon spilt over the map, even when rain started, and you began to see the lines of wool as lines of morality, linking cities of equal malice, areas of comparable level of—to use a phrase from your childhood—mortal sin. Everyone knew now—even theologians—that it was a far worse thing to use a person than to fumble with yourself in a country crapper at fourteen.

In your last corner of consciousness, you admitted to yourself: I do not love Helen, nor is it foreseeable that I will.

When you woke and turned on your side, Helen was in the room, waiting beside "Cubist" as if she had been there, like a handmaid, for perhaps an hour.

Suddenly you were afraid of such gentleness and fled into a totally predictable lust. It's her lookout, you formulated; she's fair game, you blasphemed. Beneath the nightdress the skin was very cool, suggesting she had stood a long time at an open window, debating with herself. She knows what she's doing and I certainly do, you moralized. A night for bursting ramhood and kingship. You might crack her spine or crush in her rib-cage, if that added anything.

When you had finished with her, you were very gentle and attentive, and struggled to avoid offering yourself as a reparation. Even though you yearned to punish yourself, you knew she did not deserve the final insult of compensation. In her, you feared by her silence, there was a parallel struggle not to make any further demands. You felt petulant even. Hadn't you broken in her arms? Wasn't she the winning athlete?

At last she asked you, "What was that about my nipples weeping milk?"

"What?" you said.

"I've never heard of such a thing," she seemed to complain. "You said my nipples would weep milk."

"It was a figure of speech." Why had you said such a stupid thing? Was it from the Song of Songs?

There was a silence during which you could sense how she grappled with her principles and tried not to ask the same questions women in love had always asked.

"I thought it might have arisen," she told you jovially, "from your wide experience as a lover."

"I haven't had a wide experience," you told her. And certainly it was the truth.

"Damian, did you ever know anyone whose nipples bled milk? When they were with a man, I mean?"

You said humourlessly, "I didn't know I'd be taken so literally." You had begun to fear a lovers' quarrel, for which—after the day's moral crises—you had no reserves.

Helen said, "I don't believe in the way I'm behaving."

You relented then, and kissed her breasts. You never knew: even this late you might work the trick and find yourself healthy and in love.

"Who's that?" called your father. He had heard the gate twang shut.

"What?" said Barbara.

He gave up. "Oh, hurry up with that stuff. Are you bloody manufacturing it?"

But Barbara had quietly disposed herself for your arrival. You knocked softly at the front, in the hope of not being heard. Coming in, you could not see at first—she waited on your right flank, arms folded, one hip propped on the draining-board, like a dry woman who had suffered conventionally from some guest's lateness.

The moment you saw her she surprisingly extended her hand, commanding yours. You instantly grabbed the hand with both of yours, as if you needed rescue. Yet gestures of physical affection had become an embarrassment to both of you, and after two or three seconds you returned the hand to her side. Not that the accustomed fright and exhilaration failed to arise: it was made more complex by your guilt over Helen.

"I was lucky," you said, "I got a ride the whole way from town."

"On a Saturday? You were lucky."

The father yelled, "Is that Damian? Barbara. Will you answer?"

Gesturing silence, she tiptoed to the partly opened top leaf of the veranda door and pulled it fully shut.

"Hey, what in God's name are you doing?"

Another prayer from the mother. Every time he used God's name in an unfit context the mother said a short prayer, a Glover counterweight to the Glover blasphemy. This, you knew, was a psychologically sound reaction: all signs pointed to the Glovers' destiny as corporate; they could best hope for a slight redemption.

Barbara, it seemed, felt entitled to shut them out and stand with her soft, private smile which inhabited principally her eyes and the utmost corners of her mouth. It was imperial. You had, in argument, sometimes called her the Empress Barbara. You never knew what she was smiling at and whether you were sharing a joy or being mocked.

She told you now, "They expected you last night. They were terribly hard to settle down."

"They're out there? The veranda?"

"The barn's got so musty. All this rain. Your mother nearly sat down on a black snake out there. It went whipping off down the side of the stall. *Crack, crack, crack.*"

"They aren't cold out there?"

"I've let down the canvas blinds" She displayed her remote strength and her almost-sweetness, saying, "You should have done your best to be here last night You see how it leaves them."

"I know. But people don't easily give strangers lifts any more. I must look like a psychopath or something."

"Did you pass your examinations?"

You smiled over a shiver of annoyance. "Of course. I'm your brother, aren't I? Out of pure hidebound tradition, the authorities will fail to publish the results till after Christmas."

"Barbara, how can you be so bloody inhuman?" your father called.

"You see what I mean," said Barbara. "They count the days. When you don't come it's as bad as if mathematics itself had let them down."

One of your hands appealed to reason. "Look, you can't leave the university the moment you put the last full stop on the last paper. You have to say good-bye to friends. Go to thank the tutor. Settle old debts. You're bound to these things."

"Of course." She gave the distant assent so disturbing to all the other Glovers. You could scarcely avoid wincing.

"You have to return books, you know. And have a beer here and there because Christmas is coming. There were people at the bookshop too, who'd been kind about credit—"

"Barbara!" your father roared.

"They know you're here," said Barbara without moving. She was obviously resting from their demands this morning, for her sanity's sake, or so that a given moment could be savoured. You yourself were indecently willing to delay facing them.

"How's the mother?"

"Ill, Damian," Barbara told you simply. "But not as ill as she looks or thinks she is. You'll see."

You nodded towards the syringe. "What's this?"

"Vaccination."

"Who for?"

"The mother. Against edema. We can't take risks."

"No."

With respect, you looked at the scoured sink, the gleaming kidney bowl on the draining-board, the bare surface of the table eroded by sandsoap to a landscape of ferocious hygiene.

"I should go out to them," you said.

"Just when you're ready."

"Barbara, for God's sake!" sang your father.

"You can hear it in his voice," Barbara softly commented.

"What?"

"He knows his son is home."

There was a thunderclap low down over the house, a scatter of thick summer raindrops over the roof. Barbara lifted the syringe and made for the door, towards which you yourself wavered. Her hand on the knob, she turned back with a question.

"Where did you stay last night?"

"The front of a truck. The cabin. Very comfortable."

"That's good."

"Yes. It was so bright last night. It reminded me of that time you had me recuperating out there, you remember, I had scarlet fever? You used to lie out there with me and help me make out bad similarities of camels and kings and so on in the clouds."

"Jumbos," she ventured. "I remember you were very good at spotting jumbos."

"Yes, I had a radio too. In the cabin. Popular music has gone over to songs that sound like bad verse."

"I know," she said. "Mixed metaphors."

Pity for her jolted you: how sad it must be to be the only person on Campbell's Reach who knew what mixed metaphor was. Except perhaps your father, who was also a furious self-educator.

"I don't know whether it was any better when it all sounded like Campbell's Reach Public School masturbating to drums."

You had done it: for the first time she simply laughed, and a habit her top lip had of turning up in a very young, half-worried, resistant guffaw dazzled and oppressed you, while your blood sang, with formal apologies to Helen, *Yes, this is the woman!*

"Better," she said, "if you wait here while I give the injection."

When she opened the door, bottom and top, an impression of shaded veranda entered, while more (seemingly) shoulder-height thunder rolled and big drops rattled the roof. Barbara went out.

You stood listening to the marginal voice of the fuel stove that could be heard even as the clouds burst. So too could Barbara's and her father's, both sharpened by the abrupt release of rain.

"None too soon, Barbara. What's going on?"

"Guess."

"Is Damian home?"

Barbara teased him offhandedly, yet with a ward-sister heaviness. "Damian? Do I know a Damian?"

Inside, you picked up the phial from which the syringe had been filled—something to occupy your large hands. Being a compulsive reader, you strained to make out the minute lettering. You saw immediately that the drug declared itself an antibiotic, not a vaccine. Casual interest raised your brows and brought you to the refrigerator, where you matched the phial with a pharmaceutical box on one of the shelves. In the box was a flimsy of directions which you began to read.

Meanwhile, there was the shuffle and scrape of feet from the veranda, very loud, as of perhaps half a dozen farmers.

"Now look," you heard Barbara say, "keep still."

For the first time your mother spoke. "Do you really think that stuff will do me any good?"

"Of course I do."

The feet were concentratedly still. Then there came a further scraping, a noise of propping—your mother's misbehaviour in the face of the needle.

Barbara sounded professional. "Listen, this has to go in the vein. Dad, here! Put your thumb there over the vein, will you? No, not too hard."

The mother snatched a breath in the moment of pain.

"Ah," said Barbara.

"Intravenous hurts like hell," the father conceded.

Your mother still conveyed in her voice the hurt of the needle. "I should have treatment. From a professional."

You heard Barbara murmur in her bittersweet voice, "I don't want you pestering Damian on that point. Do you understand?"

"I need every ally I can get."

"For God's sake." Barbara came close to snapping. "I think you can safely take it for granted I'm on your side."

"Any sign of the boy?" the father asked.

"I'll tell you the moment he comes."

A section of Barbara could be seen, backing through the door.

"But leave the door open," the father commanded her. "Right open."

"And listen to all your talk about Damian and professionals? No thank you."

She came inside and closed both segments of the door with emphasis, with a deft institutional firmness rather than in the spirit of the irradicable doubt and anger that infested her. At the sink she dismantled the syringe and began to boil water. In the meantime, you hid the drug flimsy in your pocket.

"You say she's well?" you whispered.

"It's all right." She patted the grumbling electric jug. "They can't hear above this. About the mother . . .?" Perhaps because it had so early been allowed to you both to see your parents as objective entities, you both used the definite article in this way—*the* mother, *the* father. "She's well enough. Better—I ought to stress this—better than she looks. She *leans* with the condition, you know, she lets it take her in any direction she wants. She has this ambition to be visited by a qualified man, a real professional. To tell him everything. How important her symptoms are. How I neglect her. I don't want to be unjust to her, but there's this television show called *Surgery Hours*. Its other title is *Dramatic Confrontations of Doctor and Patient*. She seems to get endless encouragement from it. I could shoot those television people."

Absorbed in malice towards soap opera, she did not speak again until a drop of boiling water spat from the lip of the jug onto her hand. She sniffed and switched the power off. "Listen, you didn't sleep in that truck cabin, did you?"

You at once felt a familiar weeping sensation in your stomach. A minority of your lies from the past thirteen years had survived, but you had become accustomed to have her extempore insights leap at you from every corner of the house.

"All right," you said.

"I know you." She was pouring water into a basin; and you could hear the leniency in her voice and cringe in accord.

"If you'd slept in a truck cabin you would have said it. 'I slept in a truck cabin at . . .' naming a place. You always fill in scenery when you're lying. Clouds you watched!"

"I didn't want to worry you."

She gave a small laugh that may have been ironic; if not, ever so little hysteric. "*Me* worry?"

Suddenly you found yourself angry that she so consistently saw herself as the centre of gravity in the Glover vortex of suffering. You found yourself also squaring your shoulders, as if you wanted to punch somebody. But certainly not Barbara.

"You know I value your being here all the time. No visitors."

But she had already begun to dodge out from beneath your avowals. "I have my own universe. Complete," she said.

Indeed, you had frequently seen a powerful joy suffuse her as she performed small chores of hygiene or medication— such chores as to scald a syringe and find it so easy a matter to protect your mother from infection by needle. You sensed, however, that such joy was not at work today.

"But never having the stink of the place out of your nostrils," you urged. "Rushing to town on Fridays, back home in time to see to the mother. Being *sweet* . . ." The word came out with the sound of an accusation, but you straightaway modified it. "Sweet. You *are* sweet. Being sweet to them."

"They're the conditions of our world," she said cursorily. "One of us can have a separate existence. Clearly, it has to be you. Where did you stay last night?"

In view of the ascertainable damage you had done Helen, you did not feel morally justified in pleading your separate existence. That aside, you were in any case, in a family context, overtly committed to chastity.

"I have a friend in town," you ventured.

Barbara kept chancing the tip of her second finger on the surface of her scalding bowl of water. Side by side with this office of self-punishment, she interrogated you in her blank, detached way.

"You mean you were there all the time?"

"I couldn't find a ride out this way."

"You stopped fifteen miles short. When *they* were waiting for you."

"But who comes this way late at night?"

"Mineral trucks. If you'd gone round the pubs you would have been sure to find a truck-driver coming this way."

"Well, it happens that a person feels a bloody fool walking into bars and shouting 'Who's going the beach road tonight?' "

Instantly the father shouted, "Is that Damian?"

Neither of you felt bound to answer.

"I hope you won't have to offer return hospitality."

"No, of course not. I wonder, though, if we're too concerned about them." You nodded towards the veranda. "It's becoming a different world."

"It's the same world. I see it on television."

"No, the old—you know—habits of mind are breaking down. Categories are falling apart."

"I know. The Church is falling apart—"

"You know whose fault that is," you said. A reflex humanist, you.

"It's everyone's fault. But it's the same world."

"No," you insisted. "There are actually young people who don't think in the old moulds. I know I do, but I'm not fully typical. There are really people who, in their grain, in their very—you know—*cores* don't think in terms of human or in-human, natural or unnatural. All prior judgments are suspended, as far as they're concerned."

Barbara murmured, "I know there's a lot of rebellion. Every night—"

"Not rebellion. Acceptance of things on their own terms.

You, for example. You're wasted, Barbara. Whereas the world is full of people who, if they loved a person, wouldn't give a damn if her parents were . . ."

But now Barbara had chanced her finger too deeply into the hot water, and the burn gave an edge to her answer. "What are you talking about? No love is ideal. We're cemented, you, me, them. That's what decides what you'll be—the way you're locked. You can't risk those you unavoidably love, for the sake of some possibly ideal marriage. With someone who just mightn't happen to worry that your parents are pretty heavily afflicted."

"Why didn't you tell me the truth about the syringe?" you asked her and felt in your pocket for the printed directions. It was clear that she felt harried.

"The syringe? What do you know about the practicalities of looking after a mother whose future's so uncertain?"

You shook your head, as if to clarify your motives. "I don't mention it for—you know—the sake of cancelling out my lie with one of yours. I just wonder, that's all. It sounds pretty serious. 'This preparation is classified a dangerous drug and should be administered only under expert advice.' "

Barbara spun away from the sink, folded her arms in a brisk fury. "Oh, Damian, now I'm really angry." Her black hair swayed. "Certainly the drug's an antibiotic, and certainly your mother has an infection. You'll see that soon enough. But it's mockery to ask me do I have expert advice."

You read from the flimsy. " 'Thick . . . yellowish . . . blood-tinged.' All this applies?"

"Yes. It's a dangerous enough infection. I'd thank you not to tell her, though."

Your belly leapt as your eye caught the words 'Dispose of infected bedding . . . aborted foetuses. . . .' You read them aloud in a diminished febrile voice. " '. . . and afterbirth by deep burial in quicklime.' " You cast the instructions away across the sandsoaped table, but a secret current of air spun them about and glided them back towards your hand. It was all as unreal as your own death. You clung to the obtrusive clatter of the rain, a point of reference from your (in its own way) orderly childhood. "You surely don't mean she's . . .?"

"In—in child? Of course not. The conditions exist in circumstances other than pregnancy."

Reassured, you hitched a hip onto the table and rested, but toyed once more with the sheet of directions. " 'Suspected subjects should be blood-tested. . . .' That hasn't been done?"

"Of course not." She moaned. "You know that hasn't been done."

With the rain beginning to falter, you began to dread the day that might develop, a sticky sun rolling between thunderheads, all the insects out, and lizards, in revolting frills and teguments, blinking on every second rock. And still you hadn't seen your parents.

Strength was prescriptive. No more morbid hesitancy. "I must go out and see them now," you told her.

Her hands, drawn down to her face, left her chin and revealed a regretful, unconscionably gentle smile, shared with her spread fingers, as if they actually carried some loved photograph.

"Oh, yes. You'll get an earful. 'What I need is some specialist attention, Damian. Your mother suffers something awful, Damian. Make her get help, Damian.' "

This litany, too, had reached your father on the veranda, and he called, "Hey, Barbara! What in the hell! Is that Damian?"

You felt your face give way with the helpless love and detestation you bore the three of them. Your tears broke out, your mouth was taken by a soft stammering, and you went across the room with your mute hands out. Barbara took you into her ample arms, and you were reminded by contrast of bird-boned Helen. To prevent torment spilling untidily from your mouth, you locked your lips on Barbara's shoulder; while she soothed quietly but could not supply for the inalienable duties you now must perform.

Your scattered energies rallied again. It really was, then, time to face your parents.

The veranda was fenced in and the canvas blinds, candy-striped thirteen years past (in the short summer of high Glover hopes), now bleached, had been rolled down to within inches of the fence. So the veranda light shone beneath the decreasing din of rain.

When you saw their turned faces grow vacuous with joy, the shock of their condition recurred. Throughout your adolescence, as your personality became more unified and you caught the over-all sense of your own body, their state recoiled on your mind with new harshness, a triannual concussion after a term's suspended disbelief. So central, strident, and incisive was their reality that libraries, debate, coffee in the Union, poetry, and carousings in Gamma block all seemed as removed and improbable as the life of some serf of the thirteenth century: the term-time Damian became a figure whose motives and aims were a mystery to you.

Seeing your parents, you knew that you would grow a face like theirs; the play of your face, which is a matter of habit and temperament but can be optionally controlled, would become more and more foreseeable, as desire, avidity, curiosity, and fear sank into muscles, became fixed in the bone. The fixed facial pattern of your parents' delight was as automatic and terrible as you had feared.

"Well," you told them inanely, "I got here."

Your mother, you could see, was obviously quite deformed by the infection.

3

To begin with the Glovers' first winter at Campbell's Reach:

When Barbara woke you it was scarcely any lighter than when the accustomed hornbills, flapping low over the house, had given the morning the quality of not being a time at which a young girl would die.

She said, "Damian, I've got a big favour to ask."

You could hear the brittle noises of the day's beginning: your mother at the crockery, your father stamping into his boots. Barbara herself was dressed to help with the morning milk, and you smelt the dismal soapy cleanliness of her clothes. Above all, she seemed greyer than dawn, grey from dying all night.

"Are you dying again?" you asked. You yearned to be asked to soothe or save her.

"I'm not," she said flatly, as if in withdrawal from your zeal.

A fear beset you, that she would now, after her thorough fright, become one with the household that smelt of disillusion: Mr., and before that, Corporal Glover's returned-soldier's millennium gone sour. The Pacific's splenetic victor with his Mrs. victor, joylessly in debt, belting himself to meet his poor dawn herd, and pecking tea from an anodized mug in a kitchen on the least significant of continents, the arsehole of the earth.

If there was ever a man ripe for having an onus taken from him, it was the Mr. Glover of that long postwar hiatus. The mid-fifties found him still bemused, as if his country had, meanly and behind his back, lost its virgin status; and every time he looked, it proved to him more and more thoroughly its loss of innocence. It was his fixed idea that as an old soldier, he had the right to find a sun-drugged world curled in his palm, fit for pocketing. Yet each migrant ship brought in Europe's sharp practitioners; there were too many quick brown foxes in this new era of peace: and in the year of Damian's birth the cities, all rendered primitive by striking unionists, stood convicted of their old-world ugliness.

So, home from the electric trains at dusk, from the thick breaths of Czechs and Croats, Poles and Greeks and wheeler-dealing Magyars, Mr. Glover spoke of a return to nature in far from Thoreauvian terms.

"Back to the land," he muttered over his steak charred swiftly by your mother between gasworks strikes. "Back to nature." It was a paranoid ultimatum to God and God's own country: he seemed bent on proving that they would both let him fail. Failure was, by the night Barbara bled, his mother-fluid, his poor man's emollient. What was worst was that you knew he had a certain black wit and was capable of a white one. He could not become the oaf he wanted to be. You heard him mutter things you knew by a child's instinct to be clever; but he would never sparkle at the top of his voice. He knew that society considered subtlety unpatriotic; that Mrs. Glover thought it blasphemous; and he suspected that the children might take it as a sign that they could soon expect certain family trophies ·—a sedan, a holiday cottage. To you, the children, he let himself become totally unreal, inspiredly ugly, a prodigy of madness. You respected him as you respected the thunderstorm, and far more than your concrete, harried mother praying the crisis away in some netherland of loyalties between God, her husband, and you.

That morning, Barbara was about to save his sanity, though there was as yet no indication. Last month his appeal against being refused membership of the Dairy Farmers Cooperative had been denied. His cows were inferior, deficient in butter-fat, subject to brucellosis, ticks, and bloat. The refusal infallibly handed you Glovers information about your status: you were considered one with the inbred families found entrenched all over Campbell's Reach; casual farmers, casual fishermen, mothers of their own granddaughters, fathers of their own nephews, frequenters of black gins.

So, the scraping protest of your father's boots in the kitchen. What wouldn't he do if he knew of this ultimate touch: that his daughter had bled from her private place?

Barbara said, "Wait till she goes out for wood and then burn it."

She gave you the bundled, bloodied nightdress.

The burning of clothing? "He'll give me curry."

She said no, if it came to his knowing she would stand up against him.

"Where's that bloody girl?" you could hear him saying, and were excited by the special dawn resonance of his voice and the chance of deepening his ignorance of the misfortune he had suffered in his daughter.

You took the nightdress with both hands. After she had gone you remained sitting and tensed, and your right thumb could feel the especial harshness of the cloth where blood had dried. Beginning in your shoulders, spasms of terror ran down your arms to the mere climatic coldness of your hands. How evil was

it to bleed from a private place? Was it a sin or a disease?
Would it happen often? Would it happen to you?

An especial love, shivery as your mother's methylated cure
for sunburn, vaporized from the pores of your skin. You said
her name as a pledge, and pressed the blood patch, its heavy
but natural smell, to your lips.

Your mother clopped into boots and took her blockbuster,
prized enough to have been given houseroom, from its corner.
She would split a half-dozen sections of red-box tree: her
hands, when she gave them to you, were grained with thick,
short splinters, which made you blush.

To save kerosene, the lamp had been turned out in the va-
cated kitchen. There was no room in the grate for the dress
until you had worried and broken the blazing wood. Then you
put it in, folded. But it burned badly, though the blood took
brisk fire independently of the cloth.

You had not expected the pungency of the fabric. Your eyes
watered, your hands swatted at the thick fumes. It occurred to
you that there was a special bounty in the way wood burned
so sweetly even when it came from roots deep in the foul stew
of Campbell's Reach.

When your mother came in, the cloth was two-thirds con-
sumed; its obvious odour hung over the kitchen. She rushed
to drop her armful of wood.

"What is it?" She squinted quickly into your face, into the
grate. "What is it?"

What could be said? "Barbara's nightie," you managed.

"What? What's the matter with you? Burning good clothes."

If it had been a routine evil you were doing you would have
quickly blamed Barbara. Now you could say nothing.

"It's your father and me who have to find the money. . . ."

He hated that "your father and me" as a statement of foetid
intimacy, just as you hated them to share the one set of spec-
tacles or slippers. Worse still, her exaltation was obvious, she
could best identify herself with your father by isolating in-

cidents that increased his acrid money worries. Like a nun
she could stand, her chin tucked girlishly against her chest,
while your father officiated at the heady sacraments of interro-
gation and strapping. Seven years old, you could pity her.
These were the moments when she knew she had a husband;
her marriage was verified for her, her work achieved a marital
meaning.

It seemed, when Barbara and her father came in from the cowshed at seven, that the silent ministering to the cows, the daily
sorcery that never forgot to swell even those poor udders with
milk, had given Barbara some sense of her own innocence. Your
mother had retrieved a singed remnant of the gown, a catalyst
for the father, a grandiose stage-prop by Glover standards.

"Because I told him to," Barbara called from the edge of the
solemnities.

The parents grew instantly wary, sensing sexual inferences,
and wondered now how questions could best be asked. Barbara
forestalled them.

"Because I bled all over it, half the night. I felt the blood
on my legs. It was like a bubble bursting when it started."

"All right, all right," the mother shouted. "Don't talk filthy."

A gentle and unappalled Christ, you noticed, seemed to be-
friend Barbara from his fixed place above the hearth. You felt
inclined to tell your mother of the fact, but were distracted by
your father's stunning bonhomie and by his hand on your
shoulder.

"Listen, cobber," he said, "what if you run outside. This is
woman's business."

"He knows all about it." She was terribly strong to their faces,
your astounding sister. "I didn't want to bleed all night and
think I was dying."

"All right, all right, all right," shrieked the mother. "You've
said it!"

The father was gentler, as if his child had become a young

woman, a person, your aunt—not your sister. But Barbara tossed her head; she didn't give a damn for status, but wanted to live without terror of her body.

"It's quite natural," said the mother with a tenuous gentleness. "And Damian, since you know, you'd better listen too. It's part of God's plan to make your sister a— It's part of growing up. Nothing for alarm. You shouldn't have been alarmed. Our blessed Mother will take care. . . ."

Your sister's jaws shuddered. She knew God's plan was large enough to mind itself. In the meantime she had spent the night dying. Was that just, when they could have told her, even the night before?

You could sense in your parents their caution, yet their complacency, for the cycles of nature had been affirmed in your sister's body; and a further series of physical ironies would assimilate her to them. So their gladness was obscene, and you felt intoxicated with the pure justice of Barbara's anger.

"It's still happening," Barbara said.

"That's right," the mother told them. "Every month a woman's system has this bleeding. You see, you'll be a mother one day, Barbara. And you know—your body has to be prepared and strengthened. So it has to get rid of bad material that's not any longer useful to that . . . purpose. You see?"

Instantly you made a formal peace with your mother's God, whom your father suspected of favouring Slavs; and instantly you felt sick. Bad material? you wondered. Am I poisoned? How cruel that you had always thought of blood as the mere juice of heroism, a bright accessory seeping not so torrentially from your flesh wounds as you Roy Rogered your way around the cowshed.

Then Barbara brought it home to the three of you that she had become immune from punishment. As she began to rip her clothing, none of the penny-wise slogans of the house came to your parents' lips. This was no mere waste Barbara

was committing; 'How do you think we'll find the money to
. . .?' had no validity as Barbara tore her dress, beginning at
the neck, and the cardigan, beginning at the hole on the
shoulder. You saw too that she was weeping, and that the
mother's eyes were turned aside. A phenomenon, a mighty shift
in power and authority, had occurred before your eyes.

Having expressed herself in great farting rips that showed
the yellowing rayon of her slip, she turned and ran out of
doors. Your parents followed her as if they were servants and
bound to attend. So you all stood on the back veranda and saw
Barbara loping directly west. The mother's face, turned to you,
was aghast. "Now you stay here," she said. The father had no
words, was chafing to start running.

The sun had just come up and the hill smoked softly, a
blue-white clean smoke. Downhill, beyond a wire fence that
had slackened and now lay looped and rusted in tussocks of
unsound grass, the forest shone. The bog to the southwest glit-
tered like a mineral spring. All of it came close to looking like
a place people come to for their health.

Meanwhile, Barbara was through the fence and at the edge
of the forest. Even though distance and new light had made
them sparkle like a stage set, you knew about those tea trees,
their shafts in the black-water hollows. And the leeches. Any
running away of yours, you admitted, would end well this side
of the leeches.

Your parents had now come to the grassy mire at the forest
edge and bent to spot Barbara under the branches and called
her name. When they vanished into the trees, straight in,
though unwillingly, you were startled by the rancid immensity
of their love.

The morning grew to be one of those magic periods of abey-
ance, very still, abstracted from the diverse work-loads and
orders of events that made a Monday what it was, or gave a
Wednesday its special flavor. Yet you kept the fire going, expecting rewards for being dutiful, whatever the new order

proved to be. For it would not always be cosmic holiday. Your parents would in the end return to their accustomed forms of authority; or so you supposed.

In the meantime, it was permitted you to toast large slices of tank loaf and eat them sodden with golden syrup. No one stirred the dust of the vacant road, no wind snapped the mesh of last night's dewed spiderwebs spun like a radio system between banksia tree and cowshed. The sky stood empty; the sea could be heard. Sudden teams of cormorants crackled by, and a crane, its spiny wings almost a nightmare, and the one pelican, white as a cloud, who went over each morning.

What you took as certain was that your amazing breakfast (how many slices? six? seven?) consecrated the day to a new course. On days like this, wars began, kings were beheaded, the writing went up on walls.

At noon you saw movement on the margin of the scrub—your sister stepping out into sunlight. The parents followed and appeared to have found two cows in the swamp and be leading them home. Barbara kept ahead of them, as if she were sulking or had even kept her unlikely authority. Wise enough to know you would be, in any case, subject, you ran to put wood on the fire.

After that, you ran out again to check developments, and saw your parents and the animals, and heard a rising cluck of tears which you presumed were Barbara's.

The group had come to within a furlong of the back steps when you changed all your opinions of it. Barbara was not weeping or being herded. She led. It was the mother's howling. Nor had your parents found cattle in the swamp. They had found their bovine selves, and now loped on four hoofs and had angular quarters like all the poor Glover cattle.

Your brain jangled, you felt it go cold within your skull. If you were caught seeing things like that . . .! You simply had to get over the vision, that was all. Back at the fire, you took a faggot, burnt black but very hot, and laid it in the palm of your left hand. Yelping, you felt the flesh melt and nudged the sliver back into the grate. So it was certain that your body still responded to the real.

You went and took, in fear, another look at your parents. Both were tired, as Barbara was, both clearly drained by earlier hysteria. The father still wore his grey drill shirt and old-style vest with its torn satin back. His slack arms hung either side of his bull's quarters. The mother swayed, trying to evade the issue of homecoming. Whose witchery had given her her dreadful udders?

"Go inside!" your father yelled to you.

Out of shame you did, happy if he never asked another thing of you. You plunged your burnt hand into a pot of cold water and waited. What a thing to do to a child—to let their bodily grossness, their shrouded and just-tolerable physicality fall away into the blatant limbs of cattle!

Their strange feet could be heard clopping about in the solid mud by the stairs.

"Well," you heard the father say, as if this were one of the concluding sentences in a long debate, "you'll get me the cartridges from the bedroom lowboy."

"Ridiculous," said Barbara.

Your mother was asking for her missal. But both of them sounded beyond desperation, into moroseness.

"Go over to the barn," said Barbara with a hint of tenderness. "You'll have nothing to worry about any more."

The father asked again for the cartridges. "They'd shoot a bloody man, anyhow, in this condition," he said. He seemed to have accepted half an hour or longer ago that he was in fact what he was apparently.

There was a long silence and then a shuffling, and when you looked from the window, you saw your parents trailing towards the barn in a lope of embittered obedience, their flanks such an accusation of Barbara that she was bound to snatch up a switch of pepper tree and beat them on their way.

You listened as she came up the stairs and into the kitchen, grey slime to her knees, her boots criminally sodden. But with no tribunal to answer, she took them off and put them by the stove.

"You kept the fire going," she noticed. "That's very good."

That was the finest moment. You were dizzy with gaiety.

You learned to milk. Even if you did fall asleep at midmorning, the teacher was used to it: all his school could milk and rose early for that purpose.

It took time for your parents to assimilate the practical reality of their new state, while all the time they wondered if the accident was something in their woof or a satire their minds or Barbara's mind had worked on them. When it had been so assimilated, and when Barbara's authority had been tested and found reliable, then they tended to become almost garishly human, friends who spoke too nakedly of their vulnerability. Your mind laboured to fit this new scheme of kinship. A tacit suspicion remained: that Barbara had brought on the accident out of some inspired contempt, but your parents divulged it only in moments of depression and paranoia. It had the power, always, to strike Barbara dumb.

There were questions you dreaded to have answered—your mother's lactation, your father's bovine lusts. Your chariness of answers augmented Barbara's dominance.

Barbara, you knew, kept memoirs of the new era, but the only words you wrote rose out of your wry assent to her power. Once, during your last year at high school, you were sent to supervise a junior class whose teacher was sick. An uninspired colleague of the stricken had chalked up an essay subject for the class: "My Parents—What I Owe Them, What They Owe Me."

You yourself opened a notebook and began to write compulsively.

Our parents [you wrote] brought us into the world. We owe them everything. If you asked me what we should do in return, I could best answer by telling a little story. One day my sister, suffering from a sulkiness that has to do with growing up, ran away into the swamp at Campbell's Reach. My parents followed her. It was very dim in there, and my sister hid in a place where the ground was above water, but very soggy. Still, it seemed a good place to hide. In fact, it was appalling. There were no leeches, but when you stood still, a solid skin of little sandflies would come down on your arms and legs. These little creatures are drinkers of blood. It is awesome to think that that unvisited thicket had probably been their home for centuries, that stinging blood from my sister was probably the apex of all their eons of history. They were so bad that my sister had to give her hiding place away to my parents, who were also plagued by the flies.

Well, they put her ahead of themselves and started to make their way home, away from those tiny vampires. At a certain moment, my sister turned around to them and was staggered by what she saw. Both my parents had turned into half-cow creatures. Wait there, if we're friends you won't laugh! They were like centaurs, except that the horse half was a cow half. The amazing thing was that they hadn't even noticed. They were intent on walking and the flies. To use a favoured word by writers, they were abstracted, and it had been apparently so natural for them to turn into cows, or semi-cows, or rather a semi-bull and a semi-heifer, that they hadn't suffered a second's dizziness or nausea.

The point is that my sister immediately let them know. She held no grudge, even though they had intended to punish her, for her own good. Without a second's selfish thought, she told them.

You raised your head to tell the thirteen-year-olds to keep at it.

That's the point [you then wrote]. It is the duty of a good child to let his parents know the second they turn into animals.

4

WHEN you came home from university in your twentieth year, you found Mr. and Mrs. Glover quite comfortably set up on the veranda with all the items of their peculiar freedom. Your eyes oblique, you saw first your father's chair lined with sheets of classified advertising and showing off a tin labelled THREE NUNS, which had been a Christmas present last year and had now been brought out after eleven months to mark your homecoming. There were his library books, chosen by Barbara, who knew his tastes well, his especial fondness for works that put forward long-odds interpretations of history: that Hitler was an illegitimate son of the Hohenzollerns, that Roosevelt had planned the Pearl Harbour shambles. From such reading he had built a miscellaneous knowledge of nearly quiz-king dimensions, but did his best to conceal it. He had a large library of *Reader's Digest*s and a hostility to the exploration of space.

Your mother was thinner than you could remember her ever being, and wore one of her everlasting cardigans in unvibrant pastel. Her hands toyed absently with a nasal spray, which symbolized her tendency to be a sickness bore. She had grounds for it now, though, in her appalling undercarriage.

She was a Catholic in the old mould, and in accordance had once or twice achieved a rare insight that God had chosen her out to punish in her the straying limbs of man and woman; that she was therefore elect. It was thirteen years since she had been to Mass and she thought that all latter-day talk of rebellious priests and anti-Papal bishops was a plot of Masonic–Communist origins. As late as this last winter, she had written in unspecified terms of her affliction, and in hope of a cure, to the Shrine of Saint Jude, Hope of the Hopeless, in the United States.

"Oh, Damian!" she called. She seemed to react as if you had raised a siege, and gratefully wept.

"Son," the father was muttering. "Son."

"I'm terribly sorry I'm late."

"Oh, it doesn't matter, it doesn't matter!" she howled and held out her arms categorically, drawing you in against her flat chest.

"How are you?" you asked them.

That made the mother weep a little more heartily. Your father answered for her.

"She's bad. She's in pain," he said with the solemnity he always devoted to her symptoms.

"I need a professional man," she said. To demonstrate, she turned slowly on her angular quarters. With some strain, you looked at her. A shiver ran down her sad red flanks; you could see purple knottings in her udders and the course of the violet veins that ran, noticeably distended, as far as the front legs. She moved with back legs ludicrously propped apart. You might consider shooting a mere cow that had to move like that.

Even so, you felt buffered from what you saw by an indistinct sense of the fraudulence of most of your mother's disorders, as if she had wilfully let them enter by a secret gate.

"Barbara belittles its importance," said your father. "But it's really bloody serious."

Your mother reached a large book called *The Complete Guide to Dairy Farming* from the veranda cupboard and raised it with both hands. "Page two-eighteen," she said. "Mastitis."

That was too laconic a summary for your father's taste. "But not ordinary mastitis. . . . You can't just treat it with bloody penicillin."

"No?" you sputtered, beset. "No?"

"All the symptoms are of staph infection." Your mother put the book away again, under an old lace tablecloth and a rotting edition of *Pear's Cyclopaedia*. A proud little burst of sobs broke from her. "I could die of blood poisoning. Or just of the infection."

Turning again with care, she yelped when her udders swung against the grotesque parentheses of her hind legs.

"That aside," said your father, descending from his heavy and, in its turn, somehow varnished concern for his wife, "how about yourself? God, you're a bloody big dark womanizer!"

"Now! I'm sure he's not."

"Course he is. I bet it takes more than three Hail Marys at bedtime to keep the women off him."

"Don't let him influence you, Damian. I can tell by your face that you're chaste."

You couldn't help laughing, and your father laughed too, as if he hoped it wasn't true. Already you felt the burden, however, of his hope and half-conviction that your academic life was hearty, both full-blooded and stylized, at a pitch somewhere between *The Student Prince* and *A Yank at Oxford*.

"What have you been doing up there?" he wanted to know, and nodded towards the escarpment to the west. In the first part of the nineteenth century, convicts had suspected that China lay over there. Was that a more bizarre belief than your father's assumption that European éclat and the civilized life were to be found at the tiny university up there, beyond the harsh forests of the plateau rim? "Did your head serang close down the free college? Is Alec still painting 'Prince Charles is a queer' all over the footpath?"

"Things like that." You nodded. " 'The Pope is a transvestite' —all that sort of thing."

"Trans-what?" the father asked, though he knew. It was one of those words he frequently and defensively pretended ignorance of; as if, once he admitted knowing them, he was in danger of then being asked why, knowing so much, he was a failure. He leaned back hooting, his hands on his waist. "Christ, you can't beat them!"

"That's not right." Your mother was sighing.

It was so sad that the old man actually believed *that* to be flagrant, gay, piquant. He was not a man difficult to please.

"But about the mother?" you said.

He sobered instantly. "Well, now you're here, you can call someone in."

Your mother was wheezing: all that turning and wielding of *The Complete Guide*. Was that the mastitis too, that audible congestion?

"Or you can force Barbara," said the mother. "She won't even understand, not even the pain. And it's like she can't see the veins. You know." She took on an appearance of coyness, modesty, her eyes cast down to take in the line of her own cheeks. "When she attends to me, it's excruciating. I don't have to tell you. The pain of moving . . ."

She spoke for minutes, her once firm cheeks depleted. The smell you had noticed grew an edge as she detailed everything except what you could easily read and hopelessly love in her somewhat exalted eyes: here I am (was the point her eyes made), a woman of shattering insignificance, yet twice I have had my importance verified—the accident and this sickness, whose pain is massively real and so testifies to my reality. Sometimes, as she talked, she would take up one of her patent medications—atomized mists and creams, lozenges and antacids

—and seem to take precise account of the dimensions of its tube or bottle, the nature of its packaging. To prove her desire for health, she brought out a letter from the American friar who tended the shrine to Saint Jude, Hope of the Hopeless, and who had pledged boundless spiritual resources towards her recovery from her undefined disease. You felt close to hysteria when you were given the envelope to handle, and the buff brochure with its boggling promises: "Yes, in the space age just as in other centuries, we devout clients of the saint can expect startling manifestations of his power. Kindly mark your letters, 'Attention: Father Anselm.'"

Barbara had always been tolerant, you saw, buying her the pharmaceutical fripperies with which now she fed the edges of the fire of her mastitis, writing at her dictation the letter marked "Attention: Fr. Anselm." But how could she be impervious to the clear peril of those swollen veins; how could she face it in such a low-keyed way as she had ten minutes before? And had she abstracted from the symptoms and managed not to see them, or had she decided that the thing was fatal so that fuss would merely excite the patient?

Now the rain had stammered out, and a half-emerged sun gave the distances of forest the numb sheen of anticlimax. All the frogs squealed, and the rain, dripping in gobbets from the furled ends of the blinds, made softer gutturals. Such foetid details seemed likely to seize your mind, to bring out a rash on your brain.

The mother kept speaking. "I feel like my belly might split open with the pain. There's a general dull pain around my lower parts that comes to a head every few minutes. What's the use of talking about it? I talk about nothing else to your father and Barbara. But everything's streaked with blood. And bloodclots! Even in my water. I mean, that's dangerous. It's grey. Grey with blood tints. . . ."

You looked sympathetic, since what you felt was predictably unutterable. While off-guard, you found yourself again drawn into your mother's breasts. Your head rang, for the smell of her disease came too sharply to you.

"You'd think it was the most important thing in my life," she mused. "But it isn't. You are." She kissed him with the robust suction noise that hearty mums made in old films. "Welcome home, Damian."

The father smiled. How could they be happy with the fly-ridden sun fully exposed above the house? "This pain," you said. "Who do you want to see her?"

The parents made what seemed a consolidated silence. "Someone professional. No one special. Just a qualified man."

"But—you know—he's going to find the ménage pretty—"

"Mén-who?" asked your father without sympathy.

"You know . . . the set-up. He's going to think it's strange. He might feel bound to talk about it to other experts, or to someone in authority."

You could tell from their hooded eyes that they had often enough heard the same argument from Barbara.

"We're ordinary people, son," he asserted, as a threat. "Ordinary people in need of help. How would he gain?"

"How could any professional man be so unkind?" The mother bolstered him, well practised. "It isn't as if we'd committed any crime."

"No," you admitted. You could have gone looking for the household frogs with a paling, and taught them for drumming in that niggling way. "But I thought that was why we'd gone to all this trouble—you know—led the life we've led. Because—for some damned reason—people will spend time and talent on being nasty."

There was a silence. Both parents inhaled.

"It's simpler than that, son," the father said. "Your mother needs treatment. No one should be left to suffer as she does."

"The maximum dose," stated the mother, "it doesn't sedate me any more. I wake screaming. I could scream now if I wasn't such an old hand at suffering."

"She hasn't even told us, son, that she's reached—you know —maximum sedation. She doesn't know we know. You've got to get through to her."

You paused before making a suggestion. "This new drug. Maybe it will do the trick. Give it a week or so."

"Yeah." The father spat. "Let the old bag suffer another bloody seven days!"

The mother said, "Dad! Dad!" as if she didn't, in fact, believe in naked pressure.

"Make her get a qualified man, Damian."

"I'll see what I can do," you promised them; but the father's bunched fist pounded the library books, and the THREE NUNS jumped.

"Look, it isn't the sort of case where you just see what you can do!"

"No, no. My boy will do his best. Won't you, Damian?"

In penitence, and eyes down, your father had begun to reclassify the *Digests* on his chair. You saw with longing headings such as "I Was a Castro Terrorist" and "A Revolution for Kidney Sufferers." God, couldn't you make any editorial board sit up and reach for their eighteen-point Roman!

"Look," your father was muttering. "I'm sorry, boy. I've been living with your mother's pain for three months." He brought up phlegm. You felt an urge, as he reached for a rag beside the magazines, to call out, "No, keep it and we'll analyze it. Cure may be in accessible bottles on some druggist's shelf." Yet you knew there was no hope. As you had told Helen, you had mild hopes of a cure on some psychological level.

Your father dredged the clot from his mouth quite delicately. He was a gentler man now than the blatant, hawking failure of the pre-accident days. You suffered a sudden kindred feeling for him, so innocent beside the furry and acquisitive wombs that were the mother and Barbara. And Helen, too. You remembered Helen strangely and as if she were allied to her mother. How easily, you thought, such adroit and managerial wombs outrode the illusion of male potency.

Your father was trying to work back to chatter. "And all your boozy mates! How are they? No paternity suits?"

For some reason you grew harsh. "Aren't I supposed to go and talk to Barbara?"

"Yeah. Yeah."

"Good." Already you were at the door handle, back-on to them. "It's good to be home."

Inside, all medical equipment had been tidied away. Barbara stood scouring the sink with one of those ferocious powders they put in pop-art canisters and called "Speed" or "Whiz" or "Slam." It somehow comforted you to see her plying a scouring pad, as if she had fallen away to a manageable domesticity.

She said, "I know what you've been asked to do, and I know you need explanations. All I ask is, not just at the moment."

"Barbara," you said, "it's monstrous. I've never seen anything as bad on other farms."

"Oh, it's common. Farmers don't admit to it. They hit the beast on the head."

And bury it in quicklime, you thought.

"But please, not now," she repeated.

"All right."

"Because I know we'll quarrel if we talk about it now," she threatened.

"All right. Poor Barbara."

Your hand could not stay away from her long black hair and its sweet turned-up rim. "Poor Barbara," you whispered and repeated it, catching a special fervour from the grain of her hair. Both of you stood still, but you knew she was more appalled than captivated by your stroking; while outdoors the mother squealed on a tight bubble of pain.

"Hold on to it, hold on," the father could be heard telling her.

The mother's cry of begging and thanks, tension and release, filled the kitchen.

"Don't, Damian," said Barbara at last. Meaning *Don't touch my hair.*

5

In her childhood, Barbara was allowed during illnesses to handle
some parchments in angular cursive French which her father
had picked up as a soldier one idle day in Alexandria. Mr.
Glover had gone to an Arab curio shop in search of little sandal-
wood camels for his newborn daughter, but was electrified by
the parchments, which thrilled him with a sense of his tenuous
descent from one contingent woman after another.

In buying the wad for fifteen piastres and, after worrying at
the pages with his fingers, sending them home, he was giving
his daughter something ultimately more soothing than hand-
carved beasts. About the time of the accident, Barbara could
obtain from contact with the document the same indefinite evo-
cation, never coming to a head, that her father had felt. She
became accustomed to the cursive handwriting and in her early
high-school years could identify this and that point of grammar.
The document began:

Au nom du Seigneur, ainsi soit-il!
Ici commence le procès d'examination d'une femme, Jeanne,
vulgairement dite La Pucelle, avant le Faculté Théologique
de Poitiers, et par autente Regnault de Chartres, Evêque du
Riems.

The fourteen sheets of parchment were signed

Jehanne ✠   *Pierre Seguin,*
                         Grand Bedeau de la Faculté
                         Guillaume Aymerie

From a large French dictionary, she discovered that *pucelle*
was an old word meaning Joan, the Maid of Orléans. She found
Grace James's *Saint Joan* in a library, read Bernard Shaw's play,
sensing its misrepresentations, and was lent Anatole France's
Saint Joan by a teacher. She learned that Joan spelled her name
"Jehanne" and that at her trial she had often asked that what
she called the Book of Poitiers should be produced—the record
of an examination she had faced in the town of Poitiers in
March and April 1429. It was never produced, for certain and
understandable human and political reasons, and no one knew
what had happened to it.

She knew too that Regnault de Chartres was the Archbishop
of Reims who had crowned the Pucelle's slack-grained benefi-
ciary, Charles VII of France, and that the same archbishop had
been president of the examination board at Poitiers at the time
of Joan's examination. And last of all, she could see that most
of the questions recorded on the parchment had been asked by
a Frère Seguin and Frère Guillaume Aymerie, both of whom, so
all the books said, had examined Joan of Arc at Poitiers.

These pages might be the ones Jehanne had waited for.

Barbara came to believe it with a different degree of belief at
different times. But even at fifteen she did not dream too in-
temperately. Instinct told her that tycoons might tend to fill their
high houses with death masks of Napoleon and ground plans
of the Battle of Jena; so, too, those racked by outlandish char-
isms might see themselves as Jehanne and, reading so often of

her piteous invoking of the Book of Poitiers, supply her with a copy one, two, three hundred years too late. Barbara might have thought herself of compensating Jehanne with a version in high-school French, five hundred and thirty years too late, had not chance already provided one.

She was at the same time intolerant enough of fantasy to ask herself if the document should be in French, and whether the French was of the right kind.

But beyond such detachment she allowed herself a daydream. She knew that you and she both had spiritual features that could be dressed to dazzle. Figures of mystery in European auction rooms, Hansel and Gretel from a far clearing, you shopped your magic manuscript about with peasant wiliness. An authentic Book of Poitiers, she considered, must be worth at least some hundreds of pounds sterling.

Her willingness to put a price on it showed that she had acquired in a few years a peasant attitude that Jehanne herself no doubt possessed; the conviction that mortgages, cold dawns, frostbitten chores, summer fatigues, mealtime quarrels, consecrated the family holding, made it less expendable than art treasures.

Beyond her dream of peddling the invaluable was the comfort of the manuscript. It fed Barbara with its intimations of sisterhood, its guarantee that somewhere the goodwill of those stricken with mana is recorded and cherished.

What, above all, the manuscript clarified for her was the suspicion that she herself was bound to lead an extreme and uncomfortable life of the type that is a manifestation rather than a life in its own right. She felt she must never be off parade; an uncosy super-awareness characterized her, especially in her later adolescence. She didn't like it, but she knew it befitted her. She knew that ultimately the greatest insult such a person had to face was that all around her presumed she wanted to be so marked, that she had *chosen* to transcend the warm opiates of man.

Virginity is apt in such lives that are a manifestation: religion and a sixth sense told her that. It was not apt in the young black-haired priest who came to the high school to teach Catholicism. His shallow gifts and transparent belief made him eminently corruptible—though she never found out which way his naïveté finally led him.

She was scarcely lonely, so closely could she identify herself with the Pucelle, who was fully fleshed to Barbara—not Bernard Shaw's conception of a virgin saint, but a shrew from the country, which she supposed herself to be, since she was the wearer of pants in the Glover family.

Like her father years before, she might now have been discovered fingering the letters, raking their surface for confirmations that were there, she knew, just evading her.

To save the pages from the humidity of Campbell's Reach, she sewed them up in a clear plastic sleeve.

6

To be remembered in any retelling of the Glover history was a Saturday morning in winter when Barbara was sixteen, three years after the accident. Her father had helped her milk that morning, as he often did, but had shown himself to be at the start of one of his morbid fits. Later in the morning you had both been told to tether a lowing heifer in calf to the wall of the old slab-timber shed and then to go.

But he'd need help, Barbara told him.

He said, with an old pre-accident authority, that she'd better go with you and get on with the manure work—she had managed to get a contract to supply humus to a nursery in the town. She went, disturbed by this urgent retaking of an authority on the brunt of which you were being chased out to commence digging.

The hill was still fresh with dew and grew wild daisies and

a small four-leafed blue flower that smelled of chocolate and whose name none of you ever found out, though you lived with it for all those years.

Calving was rare enough on the Glover farm and resulted from cows being placed in the south pasture, where one of Small's bulls would sometimes break the fence and do some Glover cow a service. You were innocent enough to think that perhaps your father had decided out of nicety to save you from the blunt facts of animal parturition. Not even Barbara yet understood the outlandish terrors that made him insist on privacy.

Both of you worked well, with a rhythmic peasant anonymity, your cold hands fumbling with the mouths of burlap bags. Nothing was said: your labour was its own communication.

"Who's screaming?" you asked at one time.

"Just the poor cow."

But, minutes later, you heard a scream very like a horse's, except for its thinness of pitch. Three times it rose. In the end you both ran towards it, hoping and fearing to find it the heart of some unspeakable animal tragedy. With some thirty feet still to cover, you slowed and began to stalk up to the shed: it was the equivalent of the underside of some stone you were fearful to lift.

Inside, the cow stood still and silent, though its eyes bulged warily sideways, as if on the lookout for hints of what it could best do to survive. Meanwhile, the father continued to dismember with an axe what appeared to the children to be a perfectly good bull calf. His forehoofs were wrapped about with violet entrails; a porous liver steamed at the base of a cleft in the creamy membrane that still lay all over the coat of the newborn beast. On the half-severed head shone a wide-open and detached eye of brilliant ebony gloss, the sort of eye that measures the damage done and then presents a bill.

Mr. Glover swayed a long sway and then brought his axe down on the forequarter. During the bottom half of his swing, he caught you, his children, with a corner of his eye.

"Didn't I tell you?" he called.

Barbara asked, "What are you doing?" with all her unnerving directness.

"It's my calf. To do with—"

"No, it's our calf," she told him.

"It was a monster. It had to be finished off."

Barbara made a quick count of its legs. "In what way was it a monster?"

Mr. Glover put another axe-blow into its forequarter. "I wasn't going to have it around," he puffed.

"It looks like a perfectly good calf to me," Barbara announced without mercy.

Both hands gripping the axe-handle, he raised the implement high above his head and then flung it to the ground. Then he began a hacking sob and staggered past you with his arms extended, to a point where, unnoticed by you, your mother had been standing all the time. Barbara realized much later that Mrs. Glover must have seen the butchery of the calf as a sign of the strain of his hybrid state, rather than in terms of his fear of monstrously begetting. Your mother took his head on her shoulder and stroked the lank hair.

You blushed at this unfamiliar exchange of tenderness, and your eyes reverted to the smoking ruins of the calf.

"Well you might look at that, miss!" the mother called. "It's as if you did it yourself."

"I didn't do it," Barbara said in her unemphatic way. "I wouldn't want anyone to do it. We could have sold him for a fair amount."

"You know what I mean, *miss*." She often used that word "miss." She had been a chambermaid in a city hotel where, it seemed, the housekeeper called all slackers and schemers "miss." "You know *very* well."

"I don't know," she told them, again without stress, but she was beginning to feel panic at what they might tell her.

The father raised his crumpled face from Mrs. Glover's mothering and cardiganed shoulder. "You know, you little bitch," he shrieked. "We know you made it happen."

"The calf?" she asked, in an even bewilderment most people would take for arrogance.

"Not the calf, miss. *Us.*"

"*Us*," the father shrilled. "Bloody us."

At that word, the parents turned back towards the barn, leaving Barbara and yourself to swill out the cowshed and release the delivered heifer.

Of course, you were busy telling yourself, of course she managed it, that's old news, I knew it four years ago. Then why is she standing utterly still with her handkerchief rammed between her teeth? Is she sorry for having managed it? Has she forgotten how it was done and so cannot undo it?

In fact, her parents' hysteria had struck her as a judgment, in a particular way. Now that she had heard them explicitly blame her, she felt the need to have settled the nature of her womanhood, its witchery. Did they think she could restore them by wishing it? Or did they believe that by some unknown chemistry of the womb she could make such a lasting mockery?

A doctor might know; she might respond to a particular dosage.

She remembered Joan, who had also been suspected of the mark of the beast, whatever that might be; but if fifteenth-century noblewomen were equipped to notice it, so would Dr. Fleming be, the lady doctor in town.

SOME REFLECTIONS ON THE LIFE OF JEHANNE D'ARQUE

by Barbara Glover

It is a morning in January in the wide valley of the Meuse. Even if the sun had risen, the sunlight is very thin. Mist hangs around the town, which is right down on the water-flats. Jacques', the father's, hens are pecking around the ordure-heap which is very close to the back door, too close for health's sake—no one would allow it now, not even at the blacks' camp at Burnt Bridge.

In the yard there are three or four cherry trees which are black with the cold weather.

The house is grey and still standing—according to writers. It is a square house and Jehanne's room is like a little cell.

Her father had been having dreams about Jehanne. He has dreamt that she will go off with soldiers. In those days, to go off with soldiers was a very despicable thing to do. Her father has dreamt it more than once. All the time Jehanne knows that she has to go off with soldiers, because she is suffering from her voices, the voices of three saints who have warned her that she must go on a military mission, or not so much a military mission as a mission that has to do with the morale of the French.

One writer claims that the fact that her father was dreaming her most secret thoughts was a sign of how close they were—in spirit.

Jehanne's father is interesting, because of his seriousness over her going away with soldiers. He was grim about his dreams. Imagine, dear reader, a very dark kitchen with an open hearth and a thick, crude table. At it sits her father and her two elder brothers, Jacquemin and Jean, and the younger brother, Pierre, who isn't taken into the conversation at all. Jehanne had an older sister called Catherine but by the morning I speak of, she has almost certainly died without finding out anything about her startling sister.

I can imagine the father not being too polite at the table, probably thinking nothing of bringing up wind. And the brothers spooning porridge in a way that their mouths couldn't be much closer to their bowls, and they could probably tell that the father was disturbed about Jehanne, who was about to go on a journey to her cousin, Jeanne, who was about to have a baby in a town called Burey-le-Petit.

I'm getting ahead of myself though. First about the brothers. They were made noblemen afterwards by royal charter, and no doubt their table manners improved then. But this particular morning their father was belching and breaking wind the way fathers do when they're worried. And when Jehanne was in her room, perhaps wrapping up her shifts— she was wearing an old red dress that became famous—the father was mumbling to the boys. We can imagine her wanting to cry out and ask her father did he really think she had *chosen* to hear voices, did he think anyone would really *want* to go off on a military mission? A girl likes soft treatment and doesn't want to be shot up into the heavens like a comet.

The father said, for his wife's ears and for the two older boys, "I hope Durand is strict on her." Durand was Durand Lassois, her pregnant cousin's husband. He was about forty. Jehanne could twist him round her finger. "This dream I keep having, her going off with soldiers. If I knew she was likely to go that way . . . honestly, I'd want the boys here to drown her. And if they wouldn't drown her, I would."

How Jehanne must have felt like shaking him, while he sat there judging her over his porridge. Perhaps she even wanted to say: "I am a monster, a freak, because of my visions. Do you think I chose to be, just out of pride?" She was only just seventeen. January 6th was her birthday.

Now, the next time her father met her, things were very different. She was in Reims and she even had her own page-boy and treasurer and her own priest. He knew then what going off with soldiers meant. She had actually stood at the altar with the Dauphin, whom she'd managed to bully into being crowned king. Things were different now. Maybe even he realized how lonely she must be, perched up there with her weak brother, the King—she had made him her brother by nagging—and with a jealous archbishop lowering the crown. One writer says that Jacques, the father, had to be fetched from the inn where he was staying because Jehanne was so popular that she couldn't have struggled through the crowds between her place and the inn. No doubt he watched his wind on this occasion.

She was beyond him now, because she'd become something so weird that they had to burn her (remember the nursing sister in town who was fined by the magistrate for incinerating a two-headed baby?). Because there were plenty of people on the French side that would have burnt her—Charles VII himself, that swine the Duke of Trémoille who used to take bribes from the English, and the Archbishop of Reims too.

In any case, she was weird and wonderful now, even though she was the same sane Jehanne. And her father was jolted into being himself. He stayed on at the inn, the Âne rayé, for two months after the coronation. The Âne rayé is opposite the Cathedral of Reims and Reims is a wine town. And old Mr. d'Arque had a gift of money from the king. So he stayed on for two months. Jehanne's mother must have been put out by it, because it seems as if she didn't even get to Reims for the coronation, let alone the two months of holiday at the Âne rayé, kept by a woman called Alice Moriau. I don't put down the widow's name to imply that Mr. d'Arque had much to do with the widow—all the evidence we have is against it. I just mention her name to keep Jehanne's picture real. In fact I'm sure she *is* a saint and I wouldn't want to say anything on a level that would hurt a living friend. Because I believe she is my living friend.

What I am trying to point out I'm not sure. It has a lot to do with parents not making sweeping judgments on their children. If their children have some special power of the body or mind, they didn't choose things that way. They, the parents, ought to become human at an earlier stage than they do. It takes a massive change to make them become ordinary people. It takes Jehanne to leave home in a patched red dress in January and then turn up in July in her armour and with two flags of her own carried by her own men—it takes a change like that to make her father climb down from all that rot about drowning her.

Look at all that happened to his Jehanne during the two months he spent at Reims. I don't want to offend Jehanne, and I know that she loved her father, but it's quite possible that the only drowning in the d'Arque family was old Jacques, drowned in champagne at the hotel called the Âne rayé. And why not? He'd had a hard life and he was fifty-four years old, and this amazing thing had happened to his daughter. He was very respected in his village. All the experts say that.

What I am getting at is how, in the end, parents, for all their preaching and threats, turn out to be the children. Charles VII was crowned king on July 17, 1429. I know the date backwards because it is my Jehanne's great day. Well, to get on with my point about parents, for all their talk, becoming children. From July 17, Jacques d'Arque was a boarder at a nice little inn. What was his daughter doing? (You have to remember that it was only in January that he had been mumbling into his breakfast about drowning her.) During the first four days she was trying to stop the new king taking any notice of the Burgundian envoys, whose job it was to hold up the French advance while the English marched reinforcements into Paris. Then she had to bully Charles into not slipping back to the beautiful Loire country—how I would like to see it! The Duke of Burgundy then held up the fool of a Charles by getting him to accept a fifteen-day truce, which he and the Duke of Bedford broke whenever it suited them. Jehanne wrote a letter to Reims saying how disappointed she was. Did Jacques d'Arque read it or have it read? Was it read during Mass? Did he feel helpless and sorry for her, did he feel amazed and proud? Did he shrink away and whimper? Is that why he stayed two months in the inn, sweating for news?

By the middle of August, this Jehanne who he had said he'd drown was whacking the walls of a town called Montepilloy, trying to bring on a battle, knowing that all the time Charles wasted gave the English time to build up in Paris.

Two more towns opened their gates to Charles, even though he didn't want them. He was her brother and she tried to bully him all the time so that he'd see that he was a free king, that the kingdom was waiting to fall into his lap.

Then she rode as far as St. Denis, which I believe is just a suburb of Paris these days. She rode with a man, a puzzling young man. His name was the Duke of Alençon. They campaigned together like a brother and sister, slept out in the fields often, right at the front of the army that had to drag her chosen brother the King behind it. Charles thought that if he got back to Chinon and all the shilly-shally of his court he'd be free and happy. But, by God, she had a bigger freedom than that to force on him.

Meanwhile, Mr. d'Arque is still back at the Âne rayé, drinking wine.

Then, in early September of the same year, the French army made an attack on the walls of Paris that failed. Jehanne said that she knew it would fail, her voices had told her, and while she was probing with a lance to find out how deep the water-ditch was, an arrow hit her in the thigh. The only depth old Jacques probed was the depth of a bottle. Forgive me, Jehanne, if I'm wrong. The Englishman who fired the arrow yelled out at her, "Bitch. Whore." And then he took a second shot and it went through the foot of her standard-bearer. He must have sworn, or perhaps he stopped himself, but he pulled up his visor to bend over and take the arrow out of his foot when a second, *bolt* they are rather than arrows, took him clean between the eyes and killed him on the spot.

Jehanne is led away arguing and the next day the King, led by that jealous swine La Trémoille and by the silly Archbishop, orders a withdrawal.

Meanwhile, Mr. d'Arque is only just getting round to asking for his bill to be made up at the Âne rayé. It's his daughter who has had to lose the blood and quarrel with kings and generals and suffer the voices of saints. Does she know how she works her magic? No.

So Mr. d'Arque can't punish her for it. She's bound by it, just the same as her weak brother, Charles VII. In most normal ways, it was the worst thing anyone could wish on her.

Just the same, everyone around her thinks she has *wanted* to bully her way to power. They don't see that she is the bullied one, that she has been bullied by God, who no one can stand up to. Most people think she is just trying to make an exhibition of herself.

She couldn't go immediately to town; she needed a lift from Mr. Small, a sour philanthropist who could be trusted never to do any girl of seventeen harm. At noon, every Friday in the first decade of the Glover occupation of that house, he would slow at the Glovers' gate and give one brusque croak of his horn. Even after Barbara found her own truck, his irascible goodwill made him slow as if he missed the weekly contact. And at the time of her father's quartering of the calf Barbara Glover certainly needed the transport offered.

Small was an aloof man, and his father had been the first one to settle on Campbell's Reach. He wore a grey flannel sweatshirt and had been gassed in the First War and may have seen the toppled Cathedral of Reims, no longer available for the coronation of slack boys or the eyes of the devout. Yet all he ever said was, "Your father'll have to do something about that south fence. My bulls wander over. They get tired. And the danger of bloat." And Barbara would say that yes, but it's awfully hard to sink fenceposts there, they drift loose every time it rains.

On Friday afternoons, matrons of proven deformity or malaise infested Dr. Patricia Fleming's waiting-room. They sat making low conversation or perhaps not even moving, though each seemed on the point of saying, "Of course you can be so much more open with a lady doctor, you can raise all the questions you want to."

An old lady who came to Dr. Fleming regularly ("for my needle") filled in the outlines for Barbara. "Dr. Fleming's pretty direct. Calls a spade a bloody shovel, you know. But she's terribly kind."

Frightened, Barbara had to work up spittle to manage a reply. If Dr. Fleming was so adroit at recognizing garden implements, how might she perform at reading especial signs from women's bodies?

SOME REFLECTIONS ON THE LIFE OF JEHANNE D'ARQUE

There is thought to be a deformity of a woman's body called the "mark of the beast." No one ever seemed to know what it was, but most women seemed convinced they would know it if they saw it.

Of course it was looked for on Jehanne's body.

Jehanne had to put up with many examinations, which must all have made her nervous. The first time it was the wife of the Governor of Chinon, Madame de Gaucourt, and also Madame de Trèves. This examination was made in the tower Jehanne had been given as her quarters, a tower of many one-room floors one on top of another, so that she might have thought she was starting to have some influence on the officials of the court. In fact, of course, she had to let them examine her, because she was a prisoner and knew there were many priests and others these old noblewomen had to report to.

The next time they looked at her was at Tours. She was all in a sweat to get on to Orléans with an army, but they made her answer questions from priests again, and then more women were appointed to find if she was a boy or a girl, and if she was a girl, did she have the mark, and if she didn't was she a virgin? This time it was the Queen of Sicily, the Dauphin's mother-in-law, who led the committee. Surely Jehanne was afraid. Maybe she wondered if you could have the mark through no fault of your own. And none of these old women had lived very pure lives. Who knows what mark they might see or think they'd seen?

The third time was by the Englishwoman, the Duchess of Bedford, when Jehanne was the prisoner of the English. That must have been the worst. Perhaps the Duke had tried to bully his wife into saying she'd seen the mark, or had seen that Jehanne was not a virgin. They say the Duke of Bedford watched the whole thing through a spyhole.

Anyhow, the Duchess told the truth. I suppose that's all I can ask of Dr. Fleming.

The doctor was a thin woman with a sad, pretty face. She had picked up a male brusqueness in her basically male profession.

"Well, Miss Glover," she called with a special warmth, as if she had been expecting Barbara for some months. "What's been happening to you?"

It became clear that she considered womanhood a manifold disease, and it was all just a matter of what form of infection you had.

"I think there's something wrong."

"What?"

"I don't know."

"Something gynaecological? Woman's trouble?"

"Yes."

"Poor bloody woman, eh? Do you think you're carrying a child?"

"No. I bleed," Barbara hurriedly contributed.

"Christ, I should hope so. Are you regular?"

"Yes."

"Well, we'd better have a look. Get much pain?"

She was grateful for the proffered symptom. "Yes."

"Listen, something's on your mind. Usually girls who are vague are plain pregnant. What is it?"

It was necessary to work up spittle with the tongue to make an answer. "I think there might be something wrong. Some mark on me."

"Wait on," said Dr. Fleming with all her male harshness. "You're not from that bloody Christian Motherhood crowd, are you?"

Barbara's mouth flew open, her mind emptied. Christian Motherhood was a crime she had not expected to be accused of.

"Smells just like them," the doctor said, towering at her desk. "They've been trying to set me up for years, bloody old sows. Mrs. Sharp! *Mrs. Sharp!*" Her eyes shone with a business-like vindictiveness. "We'll have a witness in."

But before Mrs. Sharp could leave the reception desk, Barbara had begun to shake her head in bafflement and tremble with defeat. The raucously sensitive doctor began to shout again. "No, it's all right. Stay there, Mrs. Sharp. Stay there.

"What do you mean by a mark?" she murmured.

Barbara knew she'd have to be explicit, unless she wanted Mrs. Sharp called in again.

"My parents are sick. They say that I'm to blame for bringing the sickness on. They think it has something to do with my womb because my first bleed brought it on."

Dr. Fleming ground her forehead into the palm of her left hand. "That's impossible! Absolutely impossible. God, sometimes I think we're in the fourteen hundreds and they only put nineteen sixty-nine on the newspapers to fool us."

"Well," said Barbara, "I know they examined Jehanne—*Joan* of Arc, you know, to see if she had any marks on her body—"

"*The mark of the beast*?" the doctor asked in a shriek.

"Yes."

"God! Firstly, your parents are wrong. Can you get them to come and see me?"

"I might be able to."

"Listen." The doctor moved up and down the surgery at a speech-making pace. "Firstly, there's no such thing as the mark of the beast. Womanhood is the mark of the beast, if you want to know. To be born a woman is to be at bay, a hunted beast from day one. A woman isn't a two-legged, baby-bearing animal. A woman, if you want my opinion, is a state of crucifixion. All right. You can undress."

Still, when the examination was made, Barbara, staring down past the ruck of her blouse, waited for the moment when Doctor Fleming would recoil in honest revulsion. The moment failed to come.

"Everything is normal, dear. All perfectly good. You keep yourself clean. And that's a very good idea. Do you have any abnormal pains, discomfort?"

"No," Barbara said doubtfully.

"Listen, tell me what the truth is, not what you think I ought to hear."

"I feel a kind of wave in my stomach. Sometimes. Like electricity."

Dr. Fleming smiled, almost regretfully. "That's perfectly natural." She faced Barbara. "Hop down." Even her perfume had a professional heaviness to it. With her mouth screwed up into one corner of her face, she seemed to Barbara to be taking stock of her own womanhood.

"Got a boyfriend?"

"No."

"You say you come from Campbell's Reach?"

"Yes."

Clearly the doctor surmised the worst of Campbell's Reach. She said, "I think you ought to have a small medical aid inserted in you. There's no charge for this medical aid, they're supplied free. But you must come back to me next month. You understand?"

Barbara knew the doctor was lying about no charge, but didn't want to hurt her or forestall the hard reverence with which she drew a plastic glove from a dispenser and took up the wire diaphragm from one of her cupboards.

"This won't hurt," she muttered, and glanced at Barbara's face for a second during which Barbara was surprised by a shiver of ambient sisterhood, because her body was of a startling importance to this suddenly saintly bowed head, was an object of service and compassion, and if a wound, then an honorable one.

"I should be serving you," she would have liked to tell the bent, intent head—though she knew Dr. Fleming wouldn't have stood for it. "This is my bleeding, open body that you respect," she wanted to tell the woman. "Are you sure you're seeing it correctly?"

"One thing's certain," Dr. Fleming muttered. "Your parents are completely wrong."

But there were marks and marks, Barbara knew. It was, at the least, a comfort to know she had no certifiable ones.

On a Friday six weeks later, when Mr. Small had brought Barbara home from her shopping, she visited her parents and, by mistake, left her mail with her mother. Returning to the barn for it a little later, she found her mother there alone and all the mail opened. She did not complain; piracy of letters was an occasional aberration of her mother's, and perhaps necessary for her health.

Among the letters the mother had illicitly read was one from Dr. Fleming. It said:

Dear Miss Glover,
    You have failed to return to me for further treatment. I told you definitely a month, and I believe it's very much to your welfare to have the device replaced, since, if it remains in place much longer, there is a strong danger of infection or sickness.
    There will of course be no charge for the visit.

"What have you let her do to you?" the mother wanted to know. She stood majestically; authority is more awesome on four legs, and she had all the grandeur of one of nature's most experienced victims.

"Nothing. I don't understand."

"You know what these devices are that doctors like this Doctor Fleming put in girls?" She explained that they were contraceptive, contrary to "Thou shalt not kill;" that Dr. Fleming had done this only because she presumed Barbara would be having evil relations with men and wanted to be sure that a child would not result.

"I see," Barbara said. It was all information. "I think it's gone now, in any case."

"Ah," said the mother, "so much for busybody Dr. Fleming."

You won't stop me liking her, though, Barbara inwardly announced.

The mother's hand took Barbara by the shoulder. "Fix me up, dear. And we'll have a little talk."

During the milking she spoke over her shoulder to her daughter; it was not, at first sight, an arrangement that allowed Mrs. Glover to speak with broad, easy wisdom. By now, though, no Glover saw any absurdity in the twice-daily burlesque of her lactation. Barbara, terrified of imminent frankness, bent concentratedly above the pail.

"You see, I'm a Catholic wife and (I'm not trying to shock you but you're getting old now) I could make use of the sort of . . . services Dr. Fleming offers—if they weren't filthy in God's eyes." She sniffed; faulty antrums made all the Glovers virtuosos of nasal wisdom and sadness.

"I think you can understand," she continued, "that I just cannot risk falling pregnant. But a person has to be a good wife too, and all the priests tell you it's mortally sinful for a wife to go on refusing and refusing." She shook her head. "Men are so different."

Barbara felt the muscles at the back of her throat clenching in readiness for retching.

"There are good Catholic methods," the mother continued, "to avoid having children—not that I didn't praise God for you and Damian, you musn't think otherwise. But these methods—they're too hard to work out for a simple woman like me."

She groaned. Barbara concentrated on the libations of good milk falling into the bucket.

The mother said, "But one thing's certain, that Dr. Fleming has befouled you without you knowing. Barbara, you must be very watchful. . . ."

7

Your room seemed not to have been touched since the past August by anything more than a light duster. Your holiday reading sat pat and gaudy on two small bookshelves made of brick and planking; and the bed was made on the clean, chaste lines of a bed in a hospital run by nuns.

All this you took account of in passing, for, having come straight from fondling Barbara's hair, you wanted to conjure fantastic possibilities by going straight to your cupboard, where you found the white overalls and gumboots, the uniform of the mineral company that mined the beach to the south of Campbell's Reach. The overalls had been thrown down, compactly folded, so that you wondered whether Barbara had laundered them as a penance, or left them alone (from either respect for your privacy, or terror of these visible implements of her loss of virginity) to settle in the folds in which you had left them.

You leaned your head against a plywood shelf and let its edge bite your forehead; a distraction from the toppling melancholy of your nonpossession of her.

The overalls dated from a Friday in the previous May. Barbara had gone to town to shop. You had gone with her, because you had agreed to meet an old schoolfriend for midafternoon beer. A cadet journalist on the town tri-weekly (which was owned by his father), the friend seemed instilled with the town's diverse life and conflicts. So that he could glance around the bar and see not simply individual men approaching more or less the human pattern but dramatic monoliths, dedicated to levees rather than dredging, to a sullage works across the river rather than to one this side. After an hour of this matching of municipal faces with their histories, you had become depressively impatient at being an alien. Your friend then had to go back to work.

You stayed on at the bar, fondling your near-empty glass in a hotel and a town which your friend had managed to estrange you from even further. Near you, a man of your own size though more taut, and with black hair that might have been Glover, called to the barmaid.

"Listen, packet of Players, love!"

The woman narrowed her eyes above the three beer glasses she was filling from a chromium beer-gun. "Can't you see I'm busy?"

The customer, who might have been Barbara's age, slowly disposed his big frame in a stance of apology.

The barmaid said, "An' I'll have less of this 'love' business. It's Mrs. Placer, thanks!"

The mineral man emphatically forwent battle with a gesture of both hands and said he was sorry. When she had gone up the bar to the cash register, he asked you did you think she thought that he had designs on her.

"She might."

"Gord! Pity poor Mr. Placer." He whistled as comment on her extreme unloveliness. "Hey, wait there, how'm I bloody well supposed to know she's Mrs. Placer?"

"I don't know. She seems to think you ought to."

"There was a young lady called Placer, got hit in the arse by some tracer."

The lady called Placer had returned to the beer-taps, where your overalled near-double swayed a little, hugging his just cause to himself.

"Hey, Mrs. Placer, love. How'm I damn well supposed to know your name's Mrs. Placer?"

"Shut up!" She pretended to be intent on the collars of the beer she was pouring. "Just shut up!"

"Listen, ask me cousin here." He clutched your elbow. "Do you think I ought to know the name of every barmaid in the bloody state?"

Shrugging, you saw the woman's face as if for the first time, the harried live liquid of her eyes set in features that it took forty semi-tropic summers and much maltreatment to make, and all that set satirically (a person would think) over the hotel uniform, the coy frilled front of her white blouse. She was frightened and pitiably ugly, you had time to see. You suggested to the Mineral Deposits man that he might forget the business.

"Yes, please," the barmaid said through clenched teeth.

But the Mineral Deposits man had gone spaciously logical. "Say, 'Yes, please, Frederic,' if we're going to be so damned fussy about names."

"Andy!" the barmaid shrieked. This last reaction had the effect on you of the splicing of the crisis of one bad film onto the doldrums of another.

Andy, you saw, was a giant who had materialized at Frederic's right side. He had hold of Frederic's elbow in a way that made him look like a formal mourner at a funeral. He waited an apparently solicitous second before bringing his fist up at great speed and into Frederic's face. Frederic fell back on your elbow and then sat on the floor.

"You too," said Andy, nodding at you. The resemblance had not evaded him.

His hypnotic fist made for your eyes with the momentum of something hurled. It seemed to you, though, that you had plentiful time to duck or dodge it; yet it had an aura that kept you still. By force of will you brought your jaw to make a left turn. The neck, under your right ear, took the blow; and that was bad enough. You told yourself that now you were entitled to fall with honour, yet found yourself still foolishly standing. Up the yellow tunnel of your vision came that fist once more.

What you next knew was that you were sitting on the floor feeling reluctantly newborn and bilious. A large head-high argument raged between Mrs. Placer, jealous Andy, and Mr. Noonan, who owned the Caledonian.

"No," Mr. Noonan was saying, "if he goes on like this every time you serve a customer, you'll just have to find a job in a frock salon or somethink."

Later, Noonan had Frederic and yourself carried to the spare room behind the kitchen, where two old iron-frame beds under homemade cotton quilts awaited vagrants or casual labourers. You could both sleep the matter off till six. If you weren't gone then, said Noonan, he would call in the police.

The door closed, and Frederic was straightaway sick in a corner. You drowsed. When you woke, it was to Frederic's inquiry: "Are you asleep?"

"I have been."

"Bloody funny. How was I to know the old whore's name?"

"As you said." You tried to stand, but the world gave you a sign of its future intentions by slipping from beneath your feet. Your mouth filled with bile.

"Did you know there's a very good whorehouse in Westcott Street?" Frederic asked.

"No. I didn't know that."

"Since we're on the subject of Mrs. Placer, like, there is one."

"Good."

"When I say good, I mean clean, anyhow."

You slept on the information. When you woke, Frederic was onto marriage.

". . . no substitute for it in the end," he was saying, garrulous with concussion. "The right kind of girl, and you'd never want Westcott Street again. You got a girl?"

"No one definite."

"No, that's me all over. No one definite for me." But he went on praising the ancient virtues; and when you woke suddenly again, it may well have been because you sensed Frederic was nearing a preoccupation you shared with him.

"You know the Beach Road? Out through Campbell's Reach?"

"Yes. I've . . . been out that way."

"There's a girl out there off one of them God-awful farms. Dark. I don't mean coloured, I mean dark-complexioned. Black hair. These big eyes. You know, they look like they're saying 'Right, mister, what are your credentials? I've been fucked around by experts.' You know the way they live out on some of them farms."

"What's her name?"

"I don't know. She drives this little blue Japanese truck. I'm driving back and forward to the refinery all day, and I suppose I only see her once or twice a fortnight. Those big eyes of hers. On high beam. You know. 'Don't you meddle with me, mister. I'll break the lead in your pencil. I'll have your balls.' And she's so bloody lovely you could bloody weep."

You shivered at the strange experience of having Barbara's harsh innocence judged as enamelled bitchery. It was as if Frederic had provoked fresh perceptions in you, so that you heard the scratching of chickens in the pub's backyard as Adam might have heard the first bird peck in triumph at the first beetle on the day of creation.

It was five o'clock. Barbara would be beginning to look for

you in pubs and the town's two depressed bookshops. But five more minutes and you would have heard the whole of Frederic's rendering of the myth he had made of Barbara.

"I reckoned she was bound to break down one day on that Beach Road and I'd pull up and fix that little Jap engine and be polite as hell, God, and restrained, you know, no chatting her up, wouldn't even notice she was a woman, that's the best way with man-eaters, they're expecting you to jump in with everything and it puts them in their place when you don't."

"She sounds ferocious," you said.

"That's how she seemed. You know. But the funny thing is I saw her in town here a few Fridays ago, and instead of being courteous and standoffish as all get-out, I fronted her straight off, like a lout. You know. I said, 'You live out on the Beach Road, don't you? I'm always passing you on the road.' I couldn't help myself. And you know what? She was kind of remote and shy herself. Spoke perfect bloody English. I was expecting her to say, 'Piss off, mister.' So she's bloody sweet as all get-out. That makes me bloody worse about her. You know, she stuck in my brain. A girl like that could be the centre of every-bloody-thing, I mean you'd have a whole bloody new world, she'd make you see everything in a new light. You know."

Frederic merged into a silence as into a burgeoning of reverence. It was incredible: for him Barbara was the untouchable essence of all reality. Yet it was in you that the novel perceptions were occurring. You felt something new secreted in you, the work of some gland that had waited twenty years for this first ejection. Under its militancy you understood poor Mr. Placer, bound by his deepest sap to his ugly woman; and were nearly coerced to explain, as bluntly as you could manage, how Frederic was disqualified on the basis that no one could possess Barbara who had not been slotted into her universe by the impact of the accident.

"Perhaps she's already married," you said.

Frederic's head shook. To deal with the objection, he turned onto his side; little-boyishly, his linked hands were held between his knees. His eyes were blank with a dark animal honesty.

"No, you can tell these things, you've seen the childbearers from these poor farms. God, you should have seen my mother—I mean, she had me when she was seventeen, and I was the second. That girl? No. And she's no whore either, because a whore wouldn't need to live on Campbell's Reach, even if she did it for five cents a throw."

Then, the question of wife/whore/spinster so acutely solved, Frederic asked you to wake him at six and closed his eyes.

You lay still in great joy, aflame with hope. A different man's desire had triggered your own.

When you left at ten past five, you took Frederic's boots with you. They rode uncomfortably, tucked under your arm.

In the department store where Barbara had an account, the mens'-wear man asked you were you starting up in a new line of work. If so, he assured you, there was three years' wear in the overalls they had in stock.

"Good," you said.

Back at the truck, which Frederic had hoped would one day do a sump or big-end within reach of his benevolence, Barbara was simmering. Half an hour late for milking. Plangent cows. Plangent mama.

"What have you got there?" she asked, making that breath-taking, tentative line of her upper lip which was one of her most powerful effects.

"Shirts," you said.

"Shirts? And the boots?"

You swung them onto the tray of the truck. "They were going for fifty cents at the Saint Vincent de Paul."

Yet for eight days afterwards you kept the overalls wrapped in your cupboard. To arrive at her door by night in Frederic's uniform was a joke that took planning: it could so easily go stale.

At the end of eight days you were beginning to see that you

must trust her to detect at the core of your fancy-dress whimsy a desire which she might be able to trick herself into contracting.

It was Saturday night. The parents were in the barn watching a documentary on Nigeria and working up a conscience over starving Ibo children. In the kitchen, Barbara was ironing clothes at one end of the scoured table. And it was at the moment that her lips pouted a little and formed themselves along half-querulous, half-questing lines, that she seemed most lovable, and you knew the time had come to initiate the masque.

You fetched the Mineral Deposits uniform and escaped with it through your window onto the veranda. In the dark your fingers trembled and you snorted at the sullenness of the press-studs. Then the unfamiliar boots, which flapped with every step you took. Past the barn, where tribal music could be faintly heard orchestrating the distant atrocities.

There was moonlight, and you waited in the deep purple shadow of the house. If the hoax failed, if she was revolted from the start, extreme action would be necessary. You might have to leave the family, or even kill yourself. Moon-eyed Frederic had brought you to this impasse.

Mounting the front stairs seemed an entirely new experience, as if the angle of your vision and the answers your emotions gave to the well-known timber were those of some stranger, some first-time visitor. *Glomp, glomp,* went Frederic's gumboots. *Glomp, glomp,* you mad bastard.

You stood in blackness, gazing at the unlit door, sniffing up the musk of the house.

You knocked. You heard her call, "Damian, can you answer that? Damian? Damian!" Then she herself was heard treading in the hallway, pausing.

"Anyone home?" you called with a sudden confidence, and all the frogs began to thunder, as if the air had conveyed certitude from you to them.

The door opened to the dark hall, where Barbara had chosen not to put a wasteful light. It was obvious that her eyes had not adjusted to the dark and that she had not seen who you were.

You introduced yourself in broad Frederic.

She stared at you while her eyes conformed to the relative brightness of the moonlight. Then she stared at your eyes to gauge their intent—ironic, picaresque, insane.

"Well," you felt safe in saying, "do I look the part?"

"What part?" she said. "You goat." But she was gazing at a meaningless point to your left now, and with a certain gaiety.

You said, "You don't know the half of it, Barbara." And, on the threshold, you told her of meeting Frederic, who was delirious with her beauty, and took on Frederic's voice again, but aggressively, and said the things Frederic had said: "Those big eyes of hers over the steering wheel, dark, you know, they say righto, mister, what are your references? I've been meddled with by experts. Eyes on high beam, I'll break the lead in your pencil, you know, and so bloody beautiful. . . ."

"Why don't you come inside," she suggested with a must-get-back-to-work vigour.

You took on gravity and your own voice again. "No, he's crazed. You're his dream. You're heaven. Honestly. The guts of creation. You're *it*." By the tone of these words you implied refusal to abandon the impersonation. "All right," she said. "I don't mind having an admirer. But listen, please come inside."

In the kitchen you could see that her eyes shone with a new recognition of you. Were women, seemingly intricate ones, endowed with a new vision of you simply on the basis of your changed clothes and accent? He had read in novels that women fell in love with uniforms. Was it now simply a matter of letting fruit fall in season? Yet she was a Christian believer in her peculiar way, and looked at incest as the vice of the lowest of valley families. And if she *was* ripe for you, she had only just now come to a knowledge of it. It was a fact that begged a little time for assimilation.

In any case, you regretted not having met oaf Frederic three

years past; that three-years-past giant and jealous Placer had
not felled the both of you.

"Don't let me interrupt your ironing," you said—in your own
voice, yet like a stranger.

She actually became girlish. "Well, sit down then."

You obeyed, and made a quizzical mouth, as if saying, "That's
right, just charades!"

What you did, in fact, was to incite her in blasphemies against
the family, timid and childish blasphemies, which you then
topped with boorish ones. You began to sweat in desire at her
pitiful impishness. There seemed little resistance to your ma-
nipulation of her; you found and exacted from her a precise
and liberating impiety. You tramped up and down like a dragoon
mad with victory and a sense of mission, and a great number
of bad, laboured, bitter jokes, which had never before been
spoken in the house, were now made—your mother's butter-fat
content, for example; your father's stud value. You improvised,
in the character of adult Frederic, the character of seven-year-
old Damian in the night-watch prior to the accident ("Put a
Band-Aid on it, sis.").

Talk took a waspishly philosophic turn. "I mean, is it—you
know—hereditary?"

"No."

"How do you know?"

"I know. In my bones."

"That's cosy. Doesn't sound like gilt-edged security to me."

"There aren't any gilt-edged securities in this life."

"Righto, righto!" you cried out, warning her off metaphysics.
"I mean, how do you know this thing hasn't happened to other
people too? I mean, the Prime Minister, Sophia Loren. They
might be able to be fixed."

"I doubt it."

"Oh, well. As long as they've had their bovine TB shots."

"Huh!" She put all her weight into a crease.

"Well, what did it? The bomb?"

"The bomb?" she said unfamiliarly. "The bomb?"

"The atom bloody bomb."

She shook her head, and behind her levity it was apparent she had never seen the accident in those impersonal terms. The bomb falleth where it will, it raineth on the just and the unjust. Whereas the accident was somehow a particularly Glover eventuality.

"Well, was it a sickness or somethink?"

"I couldn't say."

"Or did you hypnotize them, like on television, when they tell some old bag she's a duck and she tries to lay an egg?"

"You can't hypnotize people into being a—an animal. Any more than you could hypnotize your duck lady into having feathers or webbed feet."

"All right. So your mother checks herself over and finds she's a prime milker. I mean, what happened then?"

"They were angry," she said. "I don't know why." She frowned over that thirteen-year-old anger. "The cripple or the blind man or somebody who has cancer—these people aren't angry. But they—*they* were very angry."

"Who at? At you?"

"Of course at me. Perhaps they thought that if I'd only had the good manners not to mention what I saw to them, they would have stayed normal."

"And there they were: one second, two legs and two feet, joggety-jog; and the next, four hoofs et cetera. Moo!"

"Mr. Frederic," she said, "don't you think you're being very familiar?"

No doubt she had picked up the "very familiar" from her mother. However hard it was to believe that anyone, even your father, had ever been very familiar with your mother.

Nothing about this moment recommended it as the point of opportunity, but more quickly than your consciousness could take account of, you found yourself at her side, brought your hand down her hair and said, "Barbara, I'm so sick from wanting you."

She stood the iron upright and far to her left. "Damian, it isn't allowed."

For perhaps the first time ever, you cupped your hand on the skull beneath the black hair. "Do you think I'm like some Campbell's Reach oaf taking his sister while blind drunk?"

"No, I don't." She was absolutely rigid. Desire kicked in your belly: its opportunity was the fact that she had even begun to debate. "But circumstances don't alter cases."

"You bloody idiot mick," you whispered. "Circumstances make all the difference, and the circumstance is that you obsess me. I didn't choose it."

You had no idea what sort of heaven or hell you were making, yet were very optimistic. In fact, a vision came to you of a sweet, slack Barbara, smug with love, sprinting down to the surf some summer dawn when a delicate salmon haze lies over the eastern sea, rolling in breakers to wash her lovemaking off, rising with bubbles of foam in her hair.

In the event, the two of you began to make love with the vehemence of people committing an ultimate crime; yet, a second before orgasm, she seemed to become maternal. In that instant of perception you would have retracted your seed, if that had been possible.

The vision of an ample love affair vanished. She begged your pardon in unemotional terms. Then she did not speak until dinnertime on Sunday, when, as she basted the Sunday meat, you blustered at her.

"Just let me know how much longer you're going to get at me with silence?"

"I don't mean to get at you with silence, Damian. The two of us have put ourselves in debt, by our actions."

"Rubbish," you said.

"No. There's no doubt we've sinned against our ideas of good and evil."

"Not against my ideas we didn't."

"Oh, yes. That's why we used each other that dreadful way."

You roared, "What are you talking about?" That she should

talk about using people in the face of the parents' suspicions about her part in the accident was simply too perverse. "Of course people use each other on such occasions—that's the idea! Use and more than use," you admitted more softly.

"Anyhow," she said, and poured the fat of the Sabbath roast from its pan into a large and ancient fat-tin, "we're going to have to be very careful in the future. Otherwise our lives will be impossible."

Behind your clenched jaw, you had to admit she was taking it very soundly.

8

THE elder Glover could feel through his hoofs the electric contact of truck on road. A tribute to the manufacturer, he thought. To whom he immediately penned a mental letter of commendation. "Dear Sir, We have used your vehicle extensively for the transport of livestock, and my wife has never complained of her milk being turned by it—a tribute, of course, to your excellent suspension. . . ."

The excellent suspension was shuddering over corduroy road towards the beach, and Mr. Glover took the shocks in his four robust legs with gusto: all that veranda life, a chain of boredom on which were strung the spasms, flurries, medications of the day, had come close to convincing him that he should settle down to his decline. He had developed symptoms such as balled handkerchiefs, exhaustively read newspapers, catalogues of discomforts. His wife's mastitis had been obtrusive enough to distract him from his own animal potency.

"My daughter does most of our driving, over roads frequently cut by floodwater. . . ." He could see Barbara's beige elbow poking out from the window of the truck. A fallow arm, very firm, her long beige hand laid out along the dirty paintwork. Her hand in marriage . . . What a life she could have had. Mr. Glover felt exhilarated that that limb was set aside for serving the irony which was known in the house as Our Accident.

He shook the vile joy off and was then at his ease again, leaning back on the supposition that she had somehow willed the accident and could not now unwill it. She had gained in power and lost in freedom; they had gained in peace of mind and lost in status. All parties could be well advised to call it quits. Not lacking in insight, Mr. Glover knew that he would be a fool to pretend he could have coped as brilliantly as his exceptional daughter.

It was the peace of animals that Mr. Glover was most grateful for not having missed in his lifetime. Of course he had suffered exquisite despair at some notable stages of family history. But there were other times when his consciousness sank into veins, the fabric of his nerves, the organs of filtration, transmission, transformation, and cell-manufacture. He became nothing more than a walking delight in the flow of his own blood, the grandeur of its passage, the exhilaration of its oxygen. So that he came to understand why animals could stand visionary all day, drunk on the magnificence of their own livers, the splendour of their kidneys.

Into his human faculties he had no entrée. Man was cursed with mind-your-own-business vitals; his organs took revenge for his bright-boy cleverness. But even pain was different in that foursquare, shock-absorbing trunk. Pain surfaced in man with the suddenness of flotsam. But in the true animal there was a sense of nonperformance, ill performance, or overperformance in one or another function of the body. Pain came closer to being what the priests said of it: God's plan for letting us know we are ill. Still it crushed, but your complaint was more soundly, broadly based than the frightened yelp that was man's most frequent response.

The world of animal perceptions, he decided now, while thinking so genially of automobile companies—this sweet world of animal sense—had been lost to him during the damp winter month's of his wife's illness. Domestication on the back veranda. No wonder domestic pets, the really coddled ones, squinted at you with that half-begging, half-begging-off look. They had lost communication with the cosmos of their guts. Anything might happen to them, without warning, as anything happened to man.

He now rebelled against his too early abdication of his animal awareness. It was a silver if not golden afternoon, storm had backed to the mountains, and pleasant cod-liver clouds owned the east. Daughter and father topped the sandhills in their creditably well-manufactured Japanese truck and saw the long beach disappearing on both their right and left into distances clouded with a nimbus of spume.

His front hoofs pawed the floor; he felt he could take the length of that beach at the gallop. He might have toppled, so suddenly did she brake. Immediately he composed himself and scratched the shoulder his singlet left bare, scratched ruefully, on the model of old men. For his instincts were against letting Barbara know how sportive he was. There she was, climbing down from her cabin, unimpressed by her own elegance, hunting, stooped, for her sheaf of plastic bags marked STEVENS FRESH BAIT in red.

"Throw down the berley," she called.

He did—the bag of rotting fish he had travelled with.

When she dropped the tailpiece and placed a ramp for him, he stepped down with a wary gratitude, like a convalescent's.

"Snip 'em in two," he advised her. "Those worms. Stevens'd never know."

"Stevens'd know. His customers would tell him."

Stevens owned a sports store in town and sold bait. Ten of

his seaworms cost forty cents, and earned him and Barbara two cents per worm each. If she was lucky, she earned ten dollars a week from worming.

"There's a hard head at one end," she was explaining. "Customers look for it."

"But it's no good for bait."

"They still look for it."

"All right," he sang in perhaps seven or eight quavers, yielding her up to her unworldliness.

Trying to get some resonance into it, Mr. Glover coughed. "I'm going to have a swim," he announced.

"I will too," said the girl, "and work wet."

The father saw the dry olive down on her legs. "Righto," he said. "It won't do you any harm."

"What about your chest?" she asked.

"Gord!" he said.

"All right, then. Listen, I'm going to charge in."

"Like a kid?"

"Yes."

"Half your luck!"

The happy eventuality was that she sprinted ahead and left him free to enjoy the day, to snort riotously through his nostrils, to savour his eupepsia without having it used in evidence against him.

Barbara rolled in the shallows, a long scissors of a girl. She rose up dripping, and with that stare of faraway innocence which was, he thought, helped by unadmitted astigmatism.

She called something to him. For he was only a yard or so behind her, letting the flinty bubbles of foam comb his chest and belly, feeling parent-pride at the way the weight of water in her shirt forced emphasis on her excellent body.

"You got in fast," was what she was calling to him, with her glaring lack of intent.

"The air got me," he confessed, adopting the wonderment of the newly well. "It's great to be out."

Waves flopped over on their sides, with the easy slackness of voluptuaries turning over in bed, and went fizzing down his underbelly.

"I hope your mother's all right. With Damian," he soberly called to her.

Suddenly taken behind the knees by a young wave, she laughed as if tickled or even about to call out, "You damned old hypocrite!"

Barbara's bag of bad fish hissed over the wholesome, almost jellified sand like a rag over slate. At once a half-dozen small heads rose to the savoury rottenness. There was an animal quickness in Barbara's hand that jerked at a worm and had it drawn from the sand and in the bucket before Mr. Glover's fingers had got beyond a state of readiness to act.

In a second she would dismiss him from helping: she was quick at tasks and impatient of assistance, while he had been encouraged to become more and more of a blunderer in the years since the accident. He and Mrs. Glover had felt withdrawn, endowed with a serenity. In them and to them had been supremely demonstrated the folly of human self-seriousness. Their hands had accordingly begun to bumble. And it seemed that Barbara herself had sensed their exemption from labour. Both parties nevertheless suspected that his immunity had to be established by a small *pro-forma* rite of ineptitude.

The bag of offal hissed, worm heads rose, his fingers tangled with Barbara's, the worms vanished.

Mr. Glover whistled. "They're not worms. They're projectiles."

Barbara shared a fleeting smile with the sea and the easterly cloud banks. It was a habit with her: to bounce smiles or grimaces off distant natural objects.

"How about if you leave it to me?"

He yawned. "Do you want me to put them in Mr. Stevens' bags for you?"

"No. You go for a nice walk."

Again he yawned, to mask the animal freedom that surged in his belly. How he would have kicked up the sand if she hadn't been about.

"It's safer for me in the sandhills. You know."

"Good," she said in a dream, intent again on her work.

He wondered, however, if she knew about him, his weakness for heifers. Weakness? he thought. God in heaven, it wasn't a *weakness*, it was a strength, enough to drive rivets home. Perhaps she was too innocent and thought he was faithful to her mother. Perhaps her look of profound knowing was entirely a matter of a cast in her eye. Or perhaps she thought that, because he was bestial, his bestiality could not be a grave sin. Was she broadminded or innocent or simply damning him to his unspoken vice? Imagine not being sure of these basic matters, despite his years of association with her!

"Righto," he muttered. "You just honk the horn when you want to go."

Nothing in the dunes or forests could possibly detain him, he implied; he was world-weary.

Ignoring his ennui, she landed five worms in her bucket.

So he sloped off into the sandhills like an old beast looking for the necessary coalescence of moment with topography in which to die. He left his haunches slack and dragged them through the violet-flowering pigface that topped the dunes. Behind the hills, at the moist verge of the swamp, he was gaining speed on a silt surface bound by runner-grass.

Watch out for prickles! Watch out for the red-bellied snakes that had had such a damp winter for sleeping. The swing of his quarters, thump, thump, was a syncopated mystery that made gold-medallist umpteen-metre runners look sick. Fishermen, get a glance at me through the tea trees and have the bait scared from your hook. Fat-bummed mums from town, taking a risky dip in the shallows, looking out for some murderous fin to break the second line of surf ("Trevor, I told you not to let the pup in; sharks can smell dogs"), turn around and get a load of me. A load, right enough.

He reared away from a she-oak in his path and cleared his vision of women, who were not a possibility.

An episode out of *Women's Weekly*: Eric pursued Clarisse for three miles and at last convinced her that he had been de-horned and was no vision, but a living, breathing thing. While they sat in the sand, the endless pulse of the sea was matched by a growing pulse in Clarisse's breast as his animal good looks began to wreak their magic. . . .

Sour Mr. Small had a grid perhaps one and a half miles past Glovers', and grazing the headland with the rest of his herd a dozen sweet young Jerseys. Through tiny grassed hollows that brought him a view of the sea, Mr. Glover came to Small's fenced-off headland.

Below him he could see small beaches of shingle which he himself had found good for fishing in those months before the accident. Two men had come there this afternoon in tall fishing-boots and oilskins; one of them spry, the other easing himself over the basalt flanks of the hill with all the unhardihood of the hernia sufferer. Even from a distance, their tackle looked expensive—fibreglass; and their sedan, parked on the green common to Mr. Glover's right, was this year's model.

He cursed them for being there. Was the fishing so much better here than at any number of other places closer in? Were the damned jewfish milling at the feet of Small's herd? And if they were so sodding affluent—boats, tackle, and car—why didn't they buy an outboard and join the Blue Water Club, like all the other clever dicks from town?

He gathered himself behind a thicket of bottlebrush and galloped over the saddle of the road. Stretching his neck over an embankment of rank grass, he saw that old Risky-Guts, the fisherman, had seen nothing that shouldn't be. He chuckled at the grey pearliness of the sky and the distant storm-gathering mountains and had no doubt that he was king.

The risk lay with the drivers of the titanium tankers, who

might roar through the virgin scene, clattering the hell out of Small's grid, bearing the stuff of space rockets. But, paid by the load, the company's men were solid with benzedrine. A fine bull of a man could be the least of the phantasms they might see on their way through Campbell's Reach, day or night.

At the canter, he recrossed the crown of the road, carefully passed the grid, and was again among trees, a knot of scrub with sickly glossy leaves that seemed to be a mockery of holly leaves. Through them ran Small's fence and gate, which he opened. The gradual flank of the hill led him on. He could perceive an electric quiddity in the air, and knew that he would walk over the rise and find himself among cows.

He prayed for a second. Since I have already lusted and damned myself, please don't let me be disappointed.

Ah! Cropping the open places by the combed-back outline of the wood. Below them, the sea washing in and out with a passionless mastery. Some of the herd had lifted their heads, or, with a frowning petulance, gave up one tussock for another.

"All the joy gone out of grass, dearie?" he mumbled.

He advanced among them; in their sideways manner, they were all aware of him. Oh, sailor on your coastal steamer, clutch your telescope and see a trick they can't show you in Bangkok, Singapore, or Cairo.

Mr. Glover had seen some of the things they show you in Cairo when, in the name of democracy, he had visited it as Lance Corporal Glover in 1942. Reprehensible, those things, depths of malice. This was different: oysters *naturel*. He hadn't asked to be blessed with the bizarre potency of a bull.

An old cow moved across his front, eying him off. "You needn't worry, madam!" he told her. A sweet little heifer had given up grazing and stared at him in a peculiarly momentous way he had come to recognize. There lay in her eyes a sort of liquescent assent.

A minor disquiet held him back from the full flush of his sovereignty. Memory told him that he would end in feeling suicidal, eroded—an abrasive weight of disgust. God was not quite fair and played heads-you-lose-tails-I-win with the fornicator. He had the right to, since he owned the game. But it made for sadness and ashes in the mouth.

This time he would take pride in the physical achievement. We don't choose the lineaments of our needs, and from most points of view coupling was disgusting, even eating was obscene.

He came up to the heifer, whom lazy Small had not dehorned. He patted her haunches once and grabbed both horns.

Tilting the heaven over which he was king, a yellow impact knocked him to his knees. The quiescence of the young heifer, he could see, had been broken and she pivoted on her front legs. Such promptly evasive behaviour made Mr. Glover fear for a second that he had been shot.

Then he saw Small's Jersey bull a few feet away, pawing at the headland: thank Christ, Small had got round to dehorning *him*!

With a token, deal-with-you-later lunge, Small's bull stampeded the heifer and gathered himself to knock Mr. Glover further into the ground. Another impact, Mr. Glover felt certain, would burst something inside him. He watched his own panicked pale fingers scrabbling at one of the discs of conglomerate rock that were embedded all over the hillside.

"You rotten sheik bastard!" he said and let the stone tablet fall across the bull's brows. The clop of stone on bone exalted and alarmed him. An expensive noise for farmer Small.

The bull plopped to his knees, lowing urgently. Boss, boss, come and see what they're doing to your livestock. In case the damage was serious and Small could claim damages, and in case it was transitory and the bull would soon rear up again, Mr. Glover crashed into the trees and over the rise. The leaden erotic weight in his belly persisted, imperative in a way that was detached from the entirety of Mr. Glover, a fact in itself. For the rest, the harsh-edged bull had shamed him. In the haze or drone or murk of pastures he competed with beasts for a beast's prize. It was a sea of gall he sighted again at Small's gate.

If now he moved quickly, it was to avoid making Barbara blow her horn. Also, he behaved more chary of snakes, his hoofs no longer enchanted. His bones seemed still to carry the nauseous shock of Small's bull, and he pitied himself to the extent of limping.

On one point the swamp lapped close, reeds and wide islands of floating cabbage, scums of bronze, algaed reaches of fibrous grey and blue—all splendid and decayed tints, like the markings of serpents. Through its far verge ran someone's old fence, the timbers furzed over till they seemed luscious vegetables in their own right, the wire in whorls; and caught by the neck and horn in one of the wire loops, a young heifer, hip-deep and seemingly weak. She had been lowing in a peculiar plaintive manner, and perhaps had been there for days, catching bloat from eating the nitrogenous swamp weeds.

He waded to her, making faces because the bottom of the swamp seemed living fur. Once he turned his head to see his wake run gorgeously over the surface of multicoloured decay, purpled, yellowed, grey. In the snagged cow, who watched him sideways, there was no movement; she awaited him—rescue or solace—in a tremulous silence. She stayed quiet as he widened the loops and eased her head free. Yet he was too soured to search for any messages in her eye.

"Hold still," he told her.

The predictable abhorrence took him at the climax, and with it an impotence, a jolting abnegation imposed by himself at the crest of desire, with an immediate horror of the cow's body awakening to the reception of his. This was the summit of his proud afternoon, this stammer of frenzy, this pitiable epilepsy.

Dismounted, he stood for a second absolutely still. The swamp sucked and simpered in flurries around the place of their stamping rape. His cow had begun to shuffle and toss her neck luxuriously sideways.

As far as *he* could tell, he had not reached any decision about his future actions, but found his hands lunging and taking her by the horns. Immediately she began to roar but was weak from her residence in the swamp; so he sat sideways on her and felt her hindquarters give way and slop beneath the surface. She was roaring like an abattoir, but her forelegs gave way with a rush. Down you go, biddie. Her terror sucked water into her throat and she bellowed and gagged, her nose at water level. Under with her head, and her uppermost hind leg kept spiking him in the side. But a strange human righteousness kept his wrists firm: he was willing to hold her under for an hour if that was how long it would take.

Large whorls of grey water rose out of the nub of her pain and panic, but very soon the body slackened, accepted drowning with an alacrity that was nearly sad.

His singlet carried balls of hair; his coat was spiky with mud. Back at the shore, he wiped himself down, without much hope of improving his looks. Very tired, he felt, willing to die if it could be quickly arranged. Raking the hairs of his body with a literal vengeance, he thought of Damian, the crucible of hope, and began to weep.

9

THE evening of your homecoming.

You sat in the kitchen, playing with the radio. Outside, the television offered whacking haunches of sound and gravelly self-applause. Both the parents were deep in a television comedy which both pretended to detest. They seemed as unwilling to confess the jet-age expertise of the television comic as they had been, thirteen years past, to hint too early at nature's plan for girls. For both phenomena failed somehow to fit the harsh structures of their lives on Campbell's Reach.

You found on the radio band something orchestral and buoy-ant, and a documentary on watchdogs. "Heroic Rover," you muttered. The town station was sending out calls all over the valley, to people who had just lost their gall-bladders (keep the pecker up!), those smitten with love, anniversaries, or hepatitis. And one for the boys on the night shift at the valley cooperative.

How did they feel to have their names intoned on the vacant air of the valley? Did they cry, "Christ, this is death: death and howling hell and towering oblivion are a cheerio call to me, Alan Somebody, reading the gauges on the condensers at the creamery that is too good for Glover milk"?

The light was not on. The kitchen remained luminously dim beneath a new drench of rain. Barbara entered it from the hallway, wearing a detestable and preventive dressing-gown of shaggy red and white check that had once belonged to her mother. She was going to the laundry, down four steps to the west of the kitchen. There she would bathe herself in one of the washtubs, three feet off the ground, and rinse the brine and paspalum seeds off her long legs.

It may have been a form of paranoia in you; yet you felt, at moments like this one, that she intended you to remember that she had wormed and milked her heart out while you drowsed through the afternoon. You sensed that what you needed was the courage not to be too impressed by the mere quantity of her performance. Such courage you had rarely risen to. You knew that performance might simply be based on energies released in people by manner of all suspect daemons. Yet action—early rising, quantities of work—still awed you.

She sauntered a little, signifying a relaxed mood and a willingness to be consulted on this latest of Glover predicaments: the mother's staph mastitis.

"Barbara," you said. She stopped. "Barbara, it's no use pretending our reasoning hasn't let us down. We thought their life-spans would be average and their deaths sudden. But her death isn't going to be sudden." You lowered your voice. "And she stinks. You'd be used to that. But she really does *reek*. Badly."

She nodded. Her assent filled you with urgency. How could you have slept the afternoon away in the face of your mother's animal illness? Perhaps you had buffered yourself both ways, convincing yourself that there were senses in which she could not be said to be your mother, and other senses in which her mastitis was unreal—an unbroken habit of the mind, as you had told Helen. You began to speak with a new and penitential (rather than aggressive) emphasis.

"What brassy new supermarket will you buy the can in to deal with that smell?"

Wood exploded in the range and gave your sister a chance to scoop up the fragments from the floor. Such diversions suited her; she often spent whole arguments in acts of niggling house-wifeliness, pottering behind a chaste, unmocking grin with soap or curry powder or Parisian essence.

Now she stood upright with all the cinders in a dustpan in her right hand, her towel and soap in her left. She reminded you of the saying: "She really has her hands full."

"The point is," she told you, "I always take as much account as I can. You know that. So the details don't need to be mentioned now, do they?"

"But I think at the moment it's going to be a mistake to take account of *everything,* all the factors. I . . . suggest that although she *leans* in the direction of any sickness that hits her, we've reached the point where we just have to ask ourselves: Have we a sick parent now? And we have."

"I don't dispute she's sick. Listen. If you want to know, I think that early on I helped spread the infection by treating it with ointment through a nozzle. The nozzle helped spread the infection. But a person can only do what's humanly possible."

Your instincts warned you that this might be a feint: her admission of her own lack of veterinary wisdom. She might be subtly implying that she had to take into account day by day matters of such monstrousness that their weight would have crushed you. Once again, the appeal to performance!

In its own complex way, the claim angered you. You frowned with a fraudulent earnestness. "Look, I don't want to offend you. But it doesn't count for anything any more—having power over *them.* When we were young, they were demigods. They were—you know—worth dominating. But now they're only two sick old freaks."

"I don't understand what you mean. Do you think I enjoy being the boss mamma?"

You spread your hands. Secretly you were hoping she would lose her temper and her aura of detachment. "Just looking at it separately from the other motives that drive you—you know, love and concern—it sounds unbelievable that domination ought to come anywhere into it. But we can't look at our motives as if they were one simple little circle with one centre. They're millions of interlocking circles with all varieties of centres. I know you've sunk so much of your . . . young life into them. But there's still time."

"You too," she said. "You must have varieties of centres."

"I suppose so."

"And is one of them," she asked, without any rancour, "that you want to hand them over because there'll be no more responsibility then, because handing them over isn't like sending normal parents to a hospital where you'd still have to visit them and pay the bills? Because there'd be none of that if we passed them on to the authorities?"

"No, that's not true."

"But," she murmured, "if what we do has a million centres, how can anyone say yes or no?"

She waited in her prophylactic dressing-gown; twenty times more graphic than your now hazed image of Helen.

"People might lack simple motives," you told her, "but they can give simple answers to simple questions such as: Does she need help?"

"Oh, help's desperately indicated."

"Well . . .?"

She went to the telephone handset by the refrigerator. "You can do it. The town number is two-eight-three-nine, a very fine qualified man called Alexander. You call him, if you have to."

You were astounded; she knew you couldn't take decisive

action. How could you be called on to give up your parents to some stranger called Alexander at 2839?

"But it's your area," you said. "You're the only one who can brief him."

"Brief him?" She laughed quite sincerely. "No, you do it. Here you are." She cranked the tiny handle for you.

"But it's your place to . . ."

She put the receiver back. "You're free to. Whenever you like."

There you were, like some third patent person (not honest contorted Damian), some politician whose weakness everyone complained about. You were wagging your head, you knew, and blushing because of the direct, blunt way she had shown you up.

"You take it for granted," she explained, "that I can somehow inform him bit by bit, get him used to the idea. But I can't. He would have had to be here with us from the beginning to get used to it. And that's why we must go on letting her . . . simply . . . talk."

Then she went on down to the laundry and locked herself in. The radio still chattered, again predicting floods. There was no light down in the laundry. You imagined her bathing in the dark. The Empress Barbara.

You muttered ironic things about her.

The Empress Barbara takes account. As always. Amen. The benefits of the reign of the good Empress Barbara are two sec-ondhand refrigerators, one for the cowshed, one for the kitchen. In the kitchen refrigerator were two deep-frozen chickens, beer for her demon-lover Frederic, and chilled antibiotics for her to play Dr. Dan with.

Within a mere five years of the electrification of her empire, a twenty-three-inch television receiver was installed in the barn, and her subjects enjoyed continuous evening transmission. Except for a night in 1967 when a blue crane got caught in the aerial and died of eloctrocution or lack of moral fibre . . .

There was very little fun, though, in that sort of thing.

Your bedroom backed onto the veranda by a window that had

not been open for ten years. The demands of your adolescent shames and modesties had made you block it out with strips of patterned oilcloth.

At some time during the night you woke to a code of knocks on this window. Whoever it was—your insomniac father wanting talk or a cup of tea, or your mother asking for support in some seizure of pain—he had been rat-rat-tatting persistently, you had heard it in a dream as the tolling of one word, "loss," that chimed as regularly as the fist that went on knocking now. *Loss, loss, loss,* you had heard and had seen Helen's face peering at you from the flank of a Georgian clock. Wait for it, she had said. And *loss, loss, loss,* the clock had donged, waking you.

It had turned colder. You grabbed for your old windcheater with the St. Moritz badge on its biceps. *St. Moritz!* No chance of a Glover leaving jaunty bones on the ski slopes! In what fit of gaucherie, you wondered, had you bought such a thing? You supposed there was some force in the world that made you swallow all your old spasms of inane spaciousness, even if they had been suffered merely on bargain day at the Union store.

You paused now to try and rip the badge away from the garment, but the manufacturer had taken the trouble not merely to sew it there but to glue it as well. Whoever he was, he deserved bankruptcy.

As you hastened to the veranda, it occurred to you that you had never so thoroughly realized the loss of Barbara as you did now; for it seemed that sleep had made it easier for you to adjudge the imperiousness which she had been able to treat you with earlier in the night—so workmanlike, surer and more dispassionate than a lover is to a lover.

You muttered her name several times. You remembered Helen sharply, but merely for her limits, a safe wife who knew no sortilege. It would need, you understood, some twin contagion of irreducible chastity and inverted dominance to draw you free of Barbara, if freedom was what you wanted.

You found your mother alone on the dark veranda. "It's your

father," she told you. She was able to speak quite loudly beneath the gabble of the rain. "He's been gone at least half an hour. And I can see he's taken his oilskins. He said last night, while we were watching the television, that he wouldn't let Barbara use the flood as an excuse for doing nothing."

Your central preoccupation was so distant from hers that you had to ask her, "How do you mean?"

"About qualified help, of course. He's been very attentive. He wasn't always that way. But he shouldn't have gone to the extent of—"

You groaned. "Not on a night like this."

"But, as I said, that's his very point. When the flood comes on we could be cut off for a week. Ten days, even. He wants the matter settled. So do I."

"Oh, God," you said, half-mocking and fully angry. "Impetuosity."

"Now, don't go on at him too strongly. He doesn't appreciate it when Barbara goes on at him."

Your father would have taken the road to town. Along it, mineral trucks, sufficient to scatter the corpse of a stray cow every few miles, came day and night. Driving for bonuses, the drivers, drugged, and overstimulated by delivery targets, had no reason to believe their eyes or to brake for the sake of someone's stray cow.

The mother kept babbling instructions at you, and you could tell she was exhilarated by your father's gesture. Nor did she seem to consider it possible that he would actually come to the point of entering the town and clopping through its empty lighted heart in the small hours, on the lookout for some unspecified help, priest or wonder-worker, policeman or veterinary surgeon. Was it too glib of you to consider that she took your father's token escape as sufficient, that she would not care for it to go so far as to produce her cure, which would leave her bereft of her busy illness and her grievance? Perhaps, too, she saw that Barbara had always been right: isolation and secrecy were ultimately the only policy. Certainly, the more remote a figure Helen became to you, the more impossible a trust in the world's tolerance seemed.

"Use the truck," your mother recommended.

You found the keys atop the refrigerator, which hummed with a mechanical gaiety. That was progress, country-style: you had already written a short, clever poem on the point:

> NOTICE AT THE TOWN HALL
> *On the day all the fathers*
> *turn pederast,*
> *and all the mothers cannibal,*
> *uninterrupted electricity supply*
> *will be maintained.*

Outside, the rain was warm on your face, but the solid thud of it on your eyes made you frown, gave you a headache. There would be a flood, logs, breadboxes, chairs, and the gaseous shapes of dead cattle swilling into the appendix of swamp on which the Glovers lived. If they were ever to be different, an outlet had to be dug through the dunes to the sea. Glover's Inlet. The fish are running at Glover's Inlet, in the shade of the Glover Hilton.

You balanced choke against accelerator to prevent the hacking growl of the truck's imperfect mechanics, and the motor immediately started. You did not switch on the lights until you were on the road, and the areas they lit were grained solid with rain.

You drove slowly. Your lights took in the grubwhite limbs of eucalyptus and the botanical convulsions of the hated tea tree. Into such backgrounds your father would fuse only too well.

After a painstaking four miles, you turned back. The blue boles of eucalypts you mistook continually for your father's blurred face. Speed suited you now, to drive back down the road with lights low and take your lumbering father by surprise.

There was one place, about two miles from the farm, where

the road rose over a low spur of rock, a rare crest. Beyond it, the track right-angled and then ran without curving for a full mile. Coming into the right-angle corner, you had a vision of brown flanks lolloping into cover. You braked, overshooting the place, but reversed frenziedly to it and leaped out.

"All right," you yelled from the edge of the road. "All right. I know you're there." But you knew nothing—it might have been some bona fide lost cow. The numbing rain hissed over you.

"Come on," you reasoned at the top of your voice, feeling foolish. "If you want to go to town, I'll drive you. But you can't get there and back alone. The road will be cut. You know that."

You heard a sigh as the father materialized at your side. "Does Barbara know?" His sparse hair was washed diagonally across his forehead and gave the erroneous impression that he had been weeping.

"She doesn't even know. God, you're wet!"

"Wet?" he mocked. He shook his sodden flanks; there was a small slapping sound of shed water. "Well, what now?"

You thought you sensed, in the evasiveness of the question, the same reluctance you had guessed at in your mother—a devotion to the affliction rather than to the cure, to the grievance rather than its redress. Was he performing a charade or reparation for the understandable but unspeakable recourse to heifers, about which you and Barbara seemed to know without having to be told? Surely he didn't *really* want to be found at dawn in front of the Shire Offices, or be hounded past the library and the J. D. Dickson Memorial Swimming Pool? Could he *really* envisage himself, a fable, a figure of speech, an accident, groping beneath genuinely municipal light posts?

"Let's go home," you suggested. "There really isn't much time for anything else."

"Ah. She's got you tied up all ways, hasn't she?"

"That isn't the point. I mean, what were you going to do in town?"

"I hadn't made up my mind."

"It was a gesture?"

"I wanted to show strangers could have more—you know—genuine mercy than Barbara has."

"Strangers? In *that* town?"

"That's right. The time comes when you want to find out what stuff the world's made out of. Put it to the test."

You laughed. "Look, you forget what you are. So do we all, for limited periods. You're the nice Glover couple, yes. We know that. We're so used to knowing it that we forget to look at each other through a stranger's eyes."

"I've heard that sort of argument before. 'They'll make a circus of you.' As if Barbara hasn't already done that. Anyhow, I came out in the hope you'd catch up. Why don't you go on into town, even on your own?"

"I could. But I won't. Barbara's right; she knows the limits of cow-doctors. They're good citizens. A good citizen has a number of categories in his mind. He tries conscientiously to be broad-minded—that is, to put everyone he deals with into one of the categories. If he can't conscientiously manage it, whatever it is, it becomes a thing to him. To the world, you're a thing, and nothing's too bad for a thing. We mustn't risk it." There are no categories, you had told Helen; now would be the time to break the habits of mind and drive on into town with your father. But the trouble involved, the demand on the nerves, was too much for you.

"Thank you!" your father said, savagely, through his teeth. "And when your mother dies of blood-poisoning—"

You lost your temper and found yourself turning to the lit truck as if to find a weapon. "You know Barbara's doing her best. You also know being sick keeps the mother occupied. You know it all. Why don't you do the best with the situation? And come home."

"She stinks."

"I know she stinks." You were angry enough to be cruel. "For better or worse."

"Don't get so bloody parsonical."

Both of you were screaming. Suddenly your father laughed through his nose with a slow, recanting bitterness. "All right, we both know what women are."

"Do we?"

"Christ, if you grew up with Barbara, you do. They like it best when you're performing great feats that do nothing to change the way things are. So why don't you bring me struggling and bloody protesting—you know—home?"

Now you found going back nearly as unthinkable as going on. In the nausea of loss in which you had waked, you called out, "Why didn't you save both of us the trouble of getting wet?"

"It was all necessary. To keep the bloody girls happy. You'll learn, you smart know-nothing bastard."

"All right." But you could tell he was beginning to speak with an honesty that was rare between you.

"And she does stink. *You* don't have to live with it. But I want the fact bloody recorded."

"All right. Of course you don't like it."

"And while we're being so bloody Lord-Chesterfield-and-his-son with each other, what am I supposed to do with this twelve inches of mine? I'm still healthy, I've still got needs. I'd look bloody silly pulling off twelve bloody inches of myself."

"Yes," you said, almost laughing, but with your sickness of loss turning to one of pity. "Yes, I know. It's hard."

"Well, what a thing for a man to end up with, twelve inches of A-grade barmaid's delight. It could be more, for all I know. I'm no good at distances."

"I'm sorry. If you're still religious, it might help you to know that a friend of mine at the university who was in the Jesuits tells me there's a theological opinion that celibates are allowed to masturbate if they can't otherwise continue. But that's a mockery, isn't it, staying celibate at the expense of fiddling with yourself? However, I thought I'd mention it."

Your father made a noise of contempt. "Wouldn't a man

be better off if they treated him as a thing and put a bullet in him? Oh, I admit Barbara's tried to give us a sort of dignity. But every day our . . . bodies show us up."

An animal hubbub descended on you. Broad light glared over the tops of trees and then dipped to dazzle your father and show up his quarters, the hair spiked with wet. You knew by the noise that it was a mineral truck, one of the large ones with the two spaced tanks to carry the heavy titanium. It seemed to you that you smelled, and identified yourself with, the panic of the driver, who had taken the crest and corner at the highest speed he could manage, presuming a clear road but finding a truck balking him and a hallucination on the edge of the scrub. You saw a man in the high cabin, fighting with the steering, heard the high sizzle of the slewing wheels on the wet clay. The blue Glover truck was avoided, but the trailer, freighted with its tons of metal, seemed to overshoot its own cabin. The company's ten tons of truck swept sideways off the road, its left wheels pitched, and with a thunderous concussion it nuzzled its cabin nose-first into the earth. The excessive impact shook the mud beneath your feet.

"Christ," prayed the father, as if in the awed hope that metal would never again crash with such force. There was meanwhile something criminal about the impunity of the small Japanese truck, still lit and intact on the verge of the road, which you now crossed. A wheel, vast and slow as a millstone, spun above your head. Jumping to clutch the cabin door, you had it fall open with a force that came close to braining you. Befuddled wiring had turned on the cabin light, so that you could see to drop yourself on the ground inside, which was framed by the cabin's shattered windscreens. You landed by the man's forearm, severed by the windscreen's central bar. His head was face down in the moist earth. A large man, black-haired, three light creases across the solid back of his neck, olive skin. Perhaps Frederic, you crazily thought, and lifted him by the shoulders. There was no face; the front of the head had the consistency of egg yolk. You dropped the shoulders and were sick against the cabin's far wall; but looked again, feeling unfathomably to blame. The man's frame, the burrowing head, the raised buttocks, one leg kneeling, seemed the most eloquently innocent shape that could be devised.

While the Glovers (you felt) continued criminally obsessed with their family game, it was in the innocent world that the tears were shed and men grew simple-minded enough to chase bonuses through Saturday night and into Sunday morning.

"Damian," your father was calling, "watch his spine if you're going to move him."

You climbed out in a fury to prevent further oddments of army first-aid from stirring in your monstrous begetter. You could suddenly see him over the line of the door, which made a sloping platform below you.

"What do you think there is to move? You heard the impact."

He explained plaintively what damage could be done to injured people if broken bone cut their spinal cord.

You yelled at him. The spinal cord was irrelevant, you said, climbing free of the wreck with an intensity that made him flinch in expectation of a beating. Yet you could easily sense that he felt appropriately guilty and merely wanted to atone in so stressing the spinal cord. Both feeling so culpable, it was beyond you to report the accident to the company and the police; only people of less centripetal obsession were fit for such civic-minded admissions.

The rain fell with a new fervour.

"Now that we've kept the girls happy with gestures," you spat at him, "are you willing to come home?"

10

Good cover for the moonlighter Glovers, the rain spouted in veils from your farmhouse roof. You slept late under its nattering reassurance, willing to go under again every time you approached waking up to the bereaved Sunday.

Barbara could be heard when she went out at dawn, and the parents stirring ruefully. Their unexcitement told you that Barbara did not, or had chosen not to, know anything of your father's escape and recapture.

You heard her come back at seven and tune the radio in. "Flood warnings are current," you heard yet again before she turned down the volume.

"Barbara," you said over and over into your dumb pillow. It seemed to you that her shaming of you in the matter of your mother's illness, combined with the Mineral Deposits calamity, had finally deprived you of any hope of her. Your mouth was still foul from that sickness in the crumpled cabin, and Barbara's sharp name came out furry.

At last it occurred to you that officials from the company or the police would have already come, had they been coming. Some cunning clock in your brain beat more assertively and pealed you fully awake. It was already half past nine.

Immediately some texture of the air or bedclothes mysteriously recalled your experiment with overalls and gumboots last May; how your thin sister had become, the closer your wide thighs thrashed to their climax, the supervisor and witness of your convulsions, tending you through some risky seizure. That was the nature of the woman, you decided. But the memory added to your coyness as you dressed and went out to meet her.

"How is she?" you asked, coming into the kitchen.

Barbara was sawing the legs off a frozen supermarket chicken. "About the same," she said. She wore an antique pair of her father's trousers rolled up to her brown calves. "Very subdued, in fact."

You felt weak. You would have told her the whole story of the catastrophe if the telling had not been such a nervous effort.

"Any news?" you slackly asked.

"A flood," she said ironically, lifting her eyes to the clamouring roof. "Another fifty points and it'll top the levee in town."

Her knife, grating into the chicken's knees, uttered an avian squawk of savagery. "No chance of a milk pick-up from the piggery, of course. The refrigerator will get very crowded. That's the bore with floods—you have to go on milking, even if you empty the pail straight back into the mud. I did think you were going to help in the mornings."

"Yes, yes, I don't know what happened, I—I couldn't quite —you know—*face* it this morning."

"Are you embarrassed? About that telephone business? You don't have to be. I'm sure you behaved the way you did out of concern. I simply ask you to believe the same of me, that's all."

"Yes, yes, of course," you said quickly, eager to quash any comparison of sincerities.

She smiled in a muted way, a little rueful at finding you so disposed to suppress any mutual statements of motive.

There was nothing to be said as she returned a plastic bag of giblets to the refrigerator. Wholesome soup for the whole family Monday night! Country-style, as they said in the barbarous supermarkets. Next she immersed the solid little shape in a sinkful of water. Only then did she speak, to tell you to read a government letter which you would find above the refrigerator.

"It's hard to believe," she said, "but it's likely the pattern of our lives will be changed."

You found the letter.

Dear Sir [*it said*], The conversion of the dairy industry to bulk production, bulk storage and bulk pick-up is proceeding at a very marked rate, and it should not be long before a representative of our Department visits you to advise on the cost and rationalization involved in converting your property to bulk methods. Though bulk production should mean increased profit to the modern producer on a medium holding, the initial investment in freezing unit, plumbing, docking facilities and road improvement may prove, in the case of some smaller holders, beyond their financial capacity; while in the cases of others, conversion would not place them in a position in which they could expect to recoup capital outlay on the required improvements to their property. These difficulties should not, however, cause concern amongst small holders, for there will be a range of highly profitable forms of intensive farming to which they can turn. By advising the small holder on how he can best use his land in the future, and by providing him with the technical advice and the bridging finance necessary to the making of the change, this Department is determined to pursue a policy by which no farmer shall be the loser as the result of the coming

conversion. In the meantime, we invite any small holder who
has doubts about his capacity to convert to bulk production, to
write to this Department, outlining the nature of his holdings
and describing their characteristics, and to obtain details of
future probable lines of development. . . .

"I can understand you," you said, not looking at her, "ob-
jecting to becoming a—you know—an anachronism at the
age of twenty-six."

"Not only that. I don't want *them* assessed for conversion
to bulk production. Besides, what can we produce intensively
here?"

"Water lilies?" You hated your own nervous laugh.

"I can see myself as a market gardener," she mused, seeming to ignore you, "peddling watermelons on the highway. But
any other change . . ." She shrugged. "Intensive farming would
mean asking all sorts of people in, men with rotary hoes, pick-
ers, casual labourers. It's frightening."

There was no question of your saying that you would work
something out between you. Any such reassurance might make
her ironically desist from raising her eyebrows.

"They say on the radio there was a truck-driver killed on
the way into town. He has his peace," she said, quaintly con-
secrating the realities of the crushed corpse that you had
handled.

You nearly told her, fiercely, Yes, but at the price of meeting
Charon and of taking Charon's wielded oar flat on the face.

"I'm quite capable," you mumbled, "of doing the whole milk
tomorrow. You can have a rest in."

Celestial bitch and bloody angel, you thought, from some-
body-or-other's poem.

All the time keeping her eyes on the submerged chicken,
and as if she had augured the event from the disposition of
the bird's corpse, she said with her native oblique, almost apol-
ogetic omniscience, "There's someone pulling up out the front."

Jolting to the window, you saw Helen leave her parents' iridescent station wagon and work blindly on the gate latch in the undiminished rain.

"I wasn't going to let things hang all that time," she whispered without any introduction as soon as you opened the door. "Ten days of flood." She was wearing, as she often did, the university's red tracksuit, though she was, as far as you knew, no athlete. It was her travelling suit, her uniform for taking political action; it understated her prettiness and distracted males from her femininity. Or so she naïvely thought. In fact, even on this morning of stress, you could scarcely hold your hands back from feeling for the certainties of her body beneath the drooping ambiguities of the tracksuit.

"How will you get home again?" you asked her, taking almost hysterical account of the coming flood.

"That'll have to look after itself. I nearly stalled in two feet or so of water back there."

"Oh, God. Don't turn off your ignition, then."

"Too late," she sang merrily. "I already have."

"Christ! You probably won't get it going again—without a new battery and generator."

"Oh? They're more trouble than they're worth," she said of her parents' splendid beast of an automobile.

"Come in," you groaned.

She did. Her crisp and unapologetic walk took her straight into the kitchen.

"Hello," she said.

"Hello," said Barbara.

Both women looked to you emphatically for introductions. You performed them.

Helen expanded on them. "I'm the girl you telephoned Friday evening." She was bent on frankness, as if she were actually trying to sell something to Barbara. "I wasn't quite truthful then. I do know Damian quite well. I didn't know, though, whether he wanted me to mention the fact."

"Oh." Barbara towelled her hands in a secretive and unaccommodating manner; it was the mannerism of a wife caught at less than her best by one of her husband's outside interests. You cursed both of them: the way that, once they were faced with each other, everything they did was in terms of proprietorship.

Barbara was, just the same, not at her ease, being clever enough to sense the depths of Helen's cleverness. Unfortunately she did not lack the courage to be direct. "I suppose he was with you when I rang?"

"That's right. But very distressed, worried about his parents and you, but too disturbed to do anything about it, that day anyhow. He really couldn't have come home on Friday. It would have been beyond him."

"If you'd told me," Barbara said with one of her private, frugal smiles, "it would have saved me a lot of searching and delays."

"I realize that. But I felt that my first responsibility was to Damian. He was in obvious—you know—distress."

"Would you like some tea?"

"No, no. Truly. If I can get my car to start again, I'll be going soon."

She took one of the kitchen chairs and sat. So did Barbara, as if they were playing a chess game with furniture. You stood back, trying not to seem some difficult child, some third object for domination. It was worse than being discussed at the age of six by your mother and the schoolteacher, for each saw herself as both mother and teacher and was determined to have her exhaustive identity established.

"It must be very dangerous on the road today."

"About two feet deep at the worst."

"Yes. But . . ." Barbara conveyed the reservation to her hands, which twiddled a thread of towelling. "There's a floodgate over to the west that holds back all the build-up in the catchment. A time comes when the floodgate is topped and a wave of water comes down, five feet high. About five. That's when the real flood begins. You'll have to be careful."

It all reminded you, the very way they sat, of the Saturday tea parties of the years after the accident. Helen received the warning with a sporting pucker of the lips. Let flood wait until straight talkers had their say!

"I really couldn't have waited," she said, "until the floods were over to resolve my relationship with Damian."

"How do you mean, resolve your relationship?" you shouted. She nodded, as if assenting to your hatred of verbiage; and then found and used the most frightful words possible.

"I want you to marry me," she said.

Barbara jerked the thread. Her face was struck frozen with its smear of a grin.

"Oh hell," you said, shamelessly willing to convince your sister, by the quality of the contempt you could muster for Helen, that Helen was not a factor to be considered. "If you only knew the endless other matters to be 'resolved' "—you spurned the word—"before I could think of marrying anyone!"

Barbara was neither deceived nor mollified. She knew Helen's true stature; you seemed to have hoaxed yourself out of the conversation, that was all. Both of them knew you and forgave you your clumsiness.

As a matter of form, Barbara explained that as far as she was concerned it was your basic right to decide when to marry. There was no family problem that in itself made it necessary or even wise for you to delay. She laughed chastely but without intending any virginal ill-will. "It's a strange world when the boys are so backward the girls are left to do the proposing."

"Girls need to be direct now," Helen told her. "Anyway, I'm an activist by nature."

You're a squaw by nature, you considered saying, and in that no different from the girls of Aldous Huxley novels. It could have been no more maladroit to say some such thing than any of your other contributions to the dialogue had been.

"Has he given any indication of a willingness to marry you?" Barbara asked. The sentence could have been spoken by the sour maiden sister of some boy in a Chekhov short story. There was about Barbara a certain lack of what would tend to be called social sense that made her dangerous in conversation.

Helen too sensed it and inhaled strenuously. Her fine skin, that had survived all the carbohydrates of residential college kitchens, shone. "I don't," she avowed "believe in the old coupon-card system of getting engaged. By doing this, that, and the other with a girl, a man forfeits to her a number of coupons, and when she has a bookful she's earned the right to marry. A boy sleeps with a girl, for example. To some people, that's worth about two-thirds of his freedom coupons. Ridiculous! Damian has no obligations to me. All I came for was to ask him would he marry me."

A ponderous yes or no could have slipped out of your mouth like a stone, and either for reasons equally unknown to you. And that, cute radical Helen, one predestined squeak of assent, *that* was the entire coupon book.

"Just the same," Barbara was musing with farm-bred intransigence, "he must have given some sign of willingness."

"Oh for Christ's sake," you barked. "I slept with her."

"I made it impossible for you not to," Helen told you, not wanting her sexual parity to be questioned. "I made the approaches. I know that your sister might think women should be withdrawn and need to be drawn out. But really the woman ought to make the overtures, instead of letting herself be tempted to be a bitch and make a fool of the man. It's too damn profitable for a woman to be what they used to call virtuous."

It was all so pedagogic: Helen had actually gone to the trouble of being kind or arrogant enough to educate Barbara in her own moral view.

Barbara became generous and drew on her experience of worldly television dramas. "Nonetheless, surely after that, there are grounds for expecting a continued relationship?"

"I hope so," Helen admitted.

Barbara nodded. You noticed with fear her too bright, fragile willingness to acclimatize herself to the chancy world of Helen's ethical judgments. "Damian will take you in in the truck if your car won't start."

"But I mightn't get back here then," you protested.

"Isn't it only right that you take the risk?" It was hard for both Helen and yourself to tell whether her brittle alacrity had at last tipped over into mockery.

What occurred to you immediately was that you couldn't face the loss of Barbara; you feared you might even begin to beg in front of the guest. Losing Helen you could face, for the future, you felt assured, would be replete with Helens; that was, surely, statistically certain. The claim you had made on Friday to the incumbent Helen, that the Glovers were less persons in their own right than a range of relationships to Barbara was nearly true; without Barbara, you would be deprived of existence, not in the sense that you would die, but in the sense that you would be drained of significance.

You said, "I warned you, Helen, you might remember. I couldn't guarantee you anything."

"I believed you, darling." She sounded weary all at once. "It's likely to be your sister who doesn't." Again she did her sharp inhalation as a preface. "Miss Glover, you mustn't send him away. It's you he loves."

At this, to Barbara, foul insight, the evidence for which she herself possessed, your face pulsed sweat; it had been the un-utterably wrong thing to say. You cringed, seeing that Barbara had got up from her chair and come down the table. She struck Helen's upturning face. In a reflex way, Helen rose and struck Barbara back; her eyes followed her blow and came to rest on Barbara's averted face.

"If you find *that* offensive, you aren't as innocent in your mind as I am."

"That is possible," Barbara admitted softly to the far corner of the kitchen.

"Well, then." Helen showed no remorse; it was against her

platform. "I'd better go now. Damian, do you want to see me at all over the summer?"

"Hasn't she any pride?" Barbara asked the same corner of the room.

"No," said Helen. "What's pride, except a damned abstract noun? Do you want to see more of me, Damian?"

You swayed on your feet and made a face. "I ought to—" you confessed.

"But you don't."

"Not here," you whispered in a panic to get the message across, to convey your smotheration. "Not *here*, you can see that. The situation's hopeless."

"You actually have parents?"

"Yes."

She showed a wry gratitude for being given that much correct information.

"So, you might give me another spin in first term and then measure me up against . . . the home situation when you come back in May?"

She had descended at last from her attempt at sexual good sense, while Barbara still faced a corner, her shoulder turned to you. The rivalry had become more and more naked.

"I wouldn't do that. I wouldn't do that to you."

Barbara was heard. "You must take the truck, Damian. I'm sure Helen will excuse me. There's washing to do."

"Would your parents have heard all this?" Helen wanted to know before going.

"No. Well, I suppose so, yes. The . . . the gist of it. Don't worry. They want to see her win as much as they want to see her lose. I'm sorry. I never really believe how strong it all is till I get home. I never do. You buffer yourself against it and think it's been a dream. You know. Or that if you were simply more balanced, it would all appear differently. Until there you are again, right in the middle of it."

It occurred to you that what you were saying must all sound

as flat as the explanations of some faith-breaking functionary.

Nodding, Helen snatched up her keys from the table. You told her that you didn't want to lose her, that she was so strong and honest and . . . As you gazed about for an adjective, "beautiful" landed on your lips with a desperate insincerity.

"I know what I am," she told you. In repose, insidiously reasonable, she waited for you to fetch your St. Moritz jacket and take her to the gate.

There the station wagon unexpectedly fired. She waved without any of the inverted bitterness you expect of women. You wondered whether her unsurprise was ultimately worse than spitting, weeping, and reproaches. But it was certainly tidier. Good-bye, pretty delegate to the Student Power Conference. Brother Helen.

At about this time, the catchment waters nudged a bough of peppermint from the top of the sluicegate and slopped over to join the flood.

As soon as you went indoors, you could hear your father calling for you. You strode out to them; you would have been grateful for the stimulus of a quarrel.

But what they had heard had already fermented them sufficiently; your mother foamed grief down the front of her cardigan. Her udders' distended veins looked hideously purple and you resented your kinship to such a pitiable ugliness. But your father displayed a zest for his son's roguishness; last night seemed all forgotten. The parents could be as easily distracted as children.

"Oh, Damian," the mother wept. "The little slut. You shouldn't have. You can surely pray for chastity. You don't know the suffering of a mother when she hears that sort of thing about her son."

You were unkind enough to wonder if she really was so distressed. Largely, she must have been, on religious grounds alone. But through the strength of her grief she identified herself with the deceived mothers of the television serials and proved her human stature.

Your father winked and muttered, "Is she going to have a child?"

"No. She's the sort of girl who can be trusted. You know, to take precautions."

"Ah!" said the father. He smiled shyly. "There should have been more like that when I was young."

"Well, there are no end of them now," you told him bitterly.

"I'm glad someone's getting it," he said in a sort of reverence. "Hey, what was that she was saying about coupons?"

SOME REFLECTIONS ON THE LIFE OF JEHANNE D'ARQUE

Nearly everything you try to say to describe a person is a lie, because you can only say one thing about him at a time, and one thing is never the truth. So it's harder still to say in so many words how people are related to each other.

I think of Jehanne's friend, John the Duke of Alençon, two or three years older than her, but the soldier she probably saw most of.

You can put their relationship in two ways, and then ask which is which. Nobody knows. Certainly not Jehanne and the Duke.

1. The relationship of Jehanne and Alençon, idealistically speaking: He is young and believes immediately in the force of Jehanne's character. He introduces her to his wife, who has only just managed to raise the money to buy him back, at the age of eighteen, from the Anglo-Burgundians. (He was captured at the age of fifteen. She married him before puberty!) Jehanne convinces the wife and promises to bring him back safe from the campaigns that no one in authority has yet said anything about financing. So there's a touching air of vision about the first meeting of these three young people, all under twenty, two of them members of the Royal Family.

Jehanne called him her *beau duc* and once warned him about a very accurate piece of English ordnance on top of the wall of some town on the Loire, which was aiming at him. The advice saved his life.

They bivouacked together with common soldiers in the hay barns and he often enough saw her breasts, which he said were well formed, yet he had never suffered any carnal desire for her. Everyone said that, in evidence at her rehabilitation trial. Lucky Jehanne. I haven't been so fortunate, judging by some of the things men whisper to me on the streets in towns on Fridays.

Alençon is with Jehanne till the army disbands. Then after an emotional farewell, Alençon gallops home to his young wife.

2. The relationship of Jehanne and Alençon looked at in strictest realistic terms: Alençon was weak in the head, had no talents, military or otherwise. Jehanne used him to force the full pressure of her visions on the Dauphin. I don't blame her. She had a mission. But already the rich "human interest" begins to become political. All the more so because he is said to have often tried to talk Jehanne into a campaign in the West, in Normandy, where his ducal estates were in British hands. He was a flatterer of ladies, he drank too much. Someone said it is impossible to imagine Jehanne liking him except that he is married to the daughter of the Duke of Orléans. I can remember someone (I ought to keep the references, but why? I'm no scholar) saying that Joan treated him with "breezy familiarity"—some phrase like that.

Alençon had an embarrassingly husky voice and a childish sense of humour, he would believe anything and dabbled in magic. I wouldn't believe what he says about his purity at bivouacs unless it were Jehanne that was involved and unless so many tougher and better men hadn't gone out of their way to stress her sexual purity and the way they treated her as an equal rather than a girl to be taken advantage of.

In the same way, the truth of Damian, Barbara, Helen, stated idealistically: Damian is distresed at being torn between the attraction of the girl Helen and the unsolved family situation. On both sides he has been handed or has taken on certain responsibilities.

Helen is an honest, generous girl. Surely her willingness not to bind Damian is courageous.

Barbara likes Helen, is embarrassed by her cleverness, though, and by the silly slap she gives her. She wonders whether Helen is too available a person for Damian to be happy with her, or whether she is too strong for him.

The truth of Damian, Helen, and Barbara, stated realistically: Damian is unchaste. He has even committed impurities, *an* impurity, with his sister. He is willing to make use of Helen's availability, and to delay coming home on account of it.

Helen is a childish girl who is throwing herself away to any taker.

Barbara is a resentful and insincere bitch, not even as honest as Helen.

Who knows what blending of the ideal and real is the right one?

11

SHE had raised the order of her tasks to a sacramental and ritual significance, so that they had become balm and refuge to her, her surest tonic. In this way, Sunday afternoons were sacred to bait-catching. She wondered if one of the mineral trucks could take the bait to Stevens. But if the flood proved too high even for them, it didn't matter. For Sunday afternoons were consecrated to bait-catching.

She walked, finding the rain tonic too, a seal on her privacy. She carried her bright buckets, one in each hand. So close on both sides were the recurring aisles of paperbark forest that the noise of downpour came to her with a distant resonance, as if she were walking beneath some high watertight dome. Her misery ran up and down her back in fitful shivers so like small feet that she could almost believe it was domesticated, a reliant pet, hamster or possum.

The road began to mount eastwards towards dunes, shallow and melancholy; and on her right a sullen plateau of black silt, residue from the refinery, intruded on her sight, imposing a sense of raw anticlimax. A half-buried company notice warned children of cave-in and suffocation, but Barbara had never seen any child there, risking such extreme deaths.

Beyond the notice stood a long ramp of logs where an emptied tip-truck waited, its motor running. She could see the driver smoking feverishly in the cabin, and pitied him for the demands some target of deliveries was making on him. You could always tell colleagues of his, dazed with rare leisure, spending their money in a bedazzled way in town. The road took her on past him to a point where it became a shifting sandtrack through the hills.

"Hey, miss!" she heard. "Hey, miss!"

When she turned she saw that he had been following her. Now he came bouncing to her at the run. She felt no fear at all, looking clinically at his big bone-crusher fists. But while she could not fear death, she feared madness, and her head jangled as she saw, above the standard overalls and black boots, the face of Damian.

The dark eyes took her in, tentative but more obvious than Damian's. The forehead was arranged in a clumsy frown of concern, and the head had a more prognathic shape than Damian's, a narrower skull and wider jaws, carried with a blatantly false solemnity.

"I was wondering," he said, "do you live on the road there?"

"Yes. We live there."

"Oh, yeah." With obvious labour, he was creating pretexts for stopping her; she could read the signs. Innumerable men in the Friday town had stopped her first and constructed reasons afterwards. "You and your husband."

"Me and my brother."

"Oh, yeah."

"Well, if that's all you wanted to know—"

"I was just wondering if you'd seen a mate of mine go past last night."

"*Last* night." She deliberately put weight on the word to let him recall that last night had been the blindest of all.

"A mate of mine got hisself killed last night." His brow and eyes took on heavily the spurious dignity of bereavement. "He was driving a mineral trailer. You know. He went off the road just over that spur. You know."

"No," she said, "that's a long way from our place. And it was a bad night for driving, wasn't it?" She hitched one of her buckets as if about to turn and go.

"But I thought you might of noticed who else was on the road. You know. Well, my friend didn't know a thing. Went off the road. Head all caved in. You know. On impact. But the funny thing was there was a great heap of sick in the cabin." His eyes fluttered apologies for the indelicacy. "Someone must have made it. So if you saw any other traffic . . ."

"No," she said. But she suffered immediate apprehensions about that fouled cabin, for she had heard, through her sleep, the truck turn in at the gate at some improper hour. Inappropriate nausea had always been characteristic of Damian. "I'm sorry about your friend, Mr.—"

"Call me Frederic. D'you want anythink in town?" he thought to ask, frantic to keep the conversation alive. "I'm hoping to go in tonight. Don't know for sure. Transport manager's a bit edgy about my mate. You know. But if there's anythink . . ."

"No," she said with a sudden perversity, though she had all that bait to consign to Stevens. "Nothing, thanks."

She turned away and rose towards the low wracked sky, then downhill to the beach. The sea was up but seemed adulterated with grey downpour. The beach ran left and right a few hundred yards, but then was lost in an unalluring haze that the surf gave off. She was sickened to find it all so predictably dismal.

When she looked over her shoulder, the truck-driver was straggling down the dunes and trying to seem offhand, as if on some company errand. Her undisciplined heart jolted once but then remembered the long attrition it had borne. Daring him to his worst, she bent to the sand, her back to his big, strangler's hands. By the time she could sense him by her side, she had a dozen worms in her bucket.

"Listen," he said, "I know you're busy, but I've been waiting for ages for a chance to talk to you. You know?"

She stood and stared at him, as contemptuously as she could manage. It made him smile—the contempt of women reassured him. His smile was broad, dawdling, stupid, reminding Barbara of some fat Disney animal. In his eyes was an honest anxiety about being sent away.

Falsely confident, she became aware, without warning, of his heavy, direct maleness, and she felt a movement in her belly, as if her widowhood was beginning to stir and find itself uncontent. The obviously male, she saw for the first time in her life, had some relevance to her. The fact frightened her.

"I'm very flattered," she couldn't help saying, through lips that could almost be called pouting; and then, with a will, she did her private smile, which, she knew by instinct, few men ever saw among their tribes of women. She noted how much harsher her breath had become, and she thought how dangerous life must be in town or in the cities, when, despite overalls and oilskins, people's animal latencies could so thunder behind their polite faces.

She bent again to her bag of fish offal and drew it over the sand. A hateful head, furry with crawlers, rose to the taste of salt corruption. But her fingers stumbled uselessly in the sand. The head vanished.

"You've got to be quick," said Frederic. He breathed through his nose with laborious hope. "Here, I'll do some for you."

She gave up the bag to him, and he bent. His fingers showed at first a little stage fright. On his stooped back the white overalls pulled tight; she had never suspected that harsh white twill could convey so directly sexual a meaning.

"It's funny how they're always here," he said over his shoulder. "I thought I caught enough of 'em when I was a kid to wipe out the whole species. You know?"

"Did your friend have a family? The one that was killed."

"No. He was a lonesome traveller. Like me. Wait there." He drew out a particularly long worm that coiled in violet convulsions all round his blunt fingers. "Here, d'you want to have a go?"

They worked together. He applauded her successes, and she was surprised how willing she was to pose as a novice at the craft of worming. At last he stood back, supervisory, an indefinite presence at the corner of her vision. She felt giddily afraid; her breath rattled under her breastbone. She could sense, centred on this man she had fifteen minutes ago considered so limited, an ineffable spectrum of bodily possibilities.

Suddenly he put his hand on her shoulder. "What's your name, anyhow?"

"Barbara." A sexual electricity coalesced at her nipples. In some high chapel in her head she heard the challenging words "Where's your pride?" severely intoned. He raised and embraced her.

After a time, he showed himself first astounded, but then grinned widely, at finding the ground so familiar, that she was proving as direct and hungry as any number of ugly women in town. At some stage she shed her sou'wester and caped oilskin and dropped them by the buckets. They reeled together into the dunes; she knew nothing of the rain and teetered on the edge of a sand hollow.

"You right?" he asked. He was still afraid and wary of looking at her direct, as if he feared some balance might be upset.

"Oh, yes," she murmured. "The legs . . ."

She had always thought of herself as potentially a very detached lover, and what she could remember of May confirmed her suspicion, for her good intentions in the direction of abandonment had not been fully successful. Now it was appropriate for *her*, *her* rare chance, to break open, jabber, sweat, scream. A glimpse of his thighs brought to her a completely simple and unmixed will to founder on them. She babbled and begged for the play of his toil-leathered hand, she yelped for a larger intrusion. His sword-shaft-tower, hard as religion, warm as a bakery, actually held her left thigh, fencing her. She found herself clawing and crawling about to it, over flesh and sand.

She was not unaware of the variety of sexual acts. With an honest revulsion she had encountered the enthusiasm of some characters in modern novels for what she considered oral depravity. With a similar honesty—though not perhaps with unmixed motives—she had educated herself in sexual morality through a large and exhaustive work by a moral theologian, lent to Damian by the university chaplain, after his, Damian's, disturbed first year as an undergraduate. The theologian had used the term "improper receptacle (*vasa indebita*)"; and Barbara had thought of the depravities he had listed as the ultimate refuge of the degenerate. Now the unsuspected sexual meaning of her mouth broke on her; she felt both exhilarated and deliciously angry that this apparently innocent organ had lain so long undeclared within the walls of her camp. While strangled encouragements and moans escaped her glutted mouth it came to her that sexuality is man's necessary purgatory, that he can be saved through humbly digesting it. For an instant, the formula behind the accident became apparent, that she could have permanent insight into it, if only the delirium would cease a second.

She exulted that her bull from Mineral Deposits had no need of literature or theology to know what his part was. Lust was leveller and educator supreme, its culture was deposited painlessly in the blood of the literate and illiterate.

Flailing, she felt her thighs loose rivers of liquor (pink and tart and salt, she envisaged it) as his first salt seed hit her palate. She heard his bellow of release squashed by the locked softness of her hams.

The flowing ceased. There was a second's ambient repose.

Then the tough little pellet of her mind seemed to plop back into its socket. Oh, God, it begged, I am old, my thighs ache, my belly is hollowed, I am hate with a man's rubbery abomination in my mouth. The mouth she withdrew warily, as if the thing might now grow fangs and strike her. Just then Frederic, with a grin of Disneyesque fulfillment, loosed his gorged mouth from her and smiled at her around the outside of her thigh. An executioner's grin.

Such as they might have grinned over Jehanne, except that the executioner found he had to burn her entrails and heart with oil, sulphur, and charcoal, again and again all morning, but they would not be devoured. The symbolism: a heart inviolate to fire, to all the fuel in the municipality. Through the midafternoon town, the burner went running to Dominicans for absolution, after throwing the virgin's heart into the Seine. That was Jehanne.

In Barbara's case, Frederic grinned around the outside of her thigh and said, "Christ!" in confidence of future play.

She jumped out, spitting, retching, and ran up a loose, crumbling slope. Thinking she was romping, he came up behind her and wrenched her down by the hips, so that they both went slewing downhill again into the pit, like creatures into an antlion's crafty hollow. She clawed and bit, but there was nothing she could do to his coarse flesh that he didn't take as a joke.

When they rolled to a halt in their by now obtrusive nakedness, she hit him in the mouth with her closed fist. Drawing back then, he looked at her purposefully and confirmed her scowl.

"*I beg your pardon!*" he said viciously.

"Let me get dressed. And keep away from me always." She knew how mean it was, though, to pretend he had done damage which had all the time lain tacit in her.

"It'll be a pleasure," he spat. He too was testy with excess.

She began to cry without shame, and Frederic sighed. To him the experience was familiar. "Look, I'm sorry."

Her four pieces of clothing hugged to her breasts, she stumbled out of the sandtrap, hawking up traces of his seed. Reaching the sea, she washed her mouth, gargled salt water, thinner, more healthily abrasive than what she had insisted on taking into her.

She thought of suicide and of her father moping home, after some heifer, to be twice as dismally attentive to the mother. She was convinced that she had come to the far side of the illusion of desire, she had drunk down the earth. Death was the next and only possible convulsion. She sat in the shallows and let herself be rinsed by a long curling wave. She realized, grating over the sand bottom, that all experience was now altered beyond toleration. Then, still wet, she hurried into the damp comfort of her clothes.

She was drawing on the shallowly expiatory ugliness of her oilskins when Frederic arrived in the surf, dressed in swimming-trunks. Without looking her way, he strode to a point thirty yards out, where the slack between waves held him waist-deep. He dived beneath a wave and was lost to sight for a full half-minute, a deliberate absence, she thought, even a little jealously, as if he were getting some absolution not available to her; from which he certainly came back thoughtful, and wavered towards her.

At that second she felt a certain power of invocation (so she thought of it) come over her, though it was more than that, a majesty over the substance of other minds. The forgotten smell of such majesty on the morning of the accident now returned to her, its precise savour. She smelled too in Frederic the howling vacancy, the impoverished suggestibility, the paltriness of malice she had identified in her parents. *I brought it off,* she exulted in terror, knowing she couldn't outlive the knowledge. Yet this time, she could not prevent herself from hoping, I might acquire the knack in a more lasting manner.

"Go away," she called. "Quickly." Lest her mind take its offhand lunge at his.

He was startled, sure enough, found it alarmingly unlike the standard brushoff.

"What are you trying to—" he began.

She screamed warnings at him. He stared slowly down his body, expecting something monstrous. Unenlightened by the survey, he frowned again. A viable parody of him jolted at the limits of her consciousness, as if she possessed the ability to impose new forms. She was shaken by a loathing for such creativity, and grew strident, still warning him when he had turned and begun to quick-walk, then jog away inland. He was urgently embarrassed or afraid, and she laughed when she saw him sprint up the dunes, his legs striking out widely on the crumbling hill.

"How is it done?" she screamed, scattering coward gulls who had swept in at the tang of her berley. She felt certain that, by some half-accidental exercise of rune of the type that had consecrated her to her parents, she had been about to add Frederic to the Glover circus.

You woke with a shock early that afternoon to find yourself captured whole by a dreadful love for your parents. Your father's second or two of gracious self-mockery that morning seemed grounds for acquittal from the evasions and horrendous animal scufflings of the past. Your mother's pain was purply real in your mind, and her grief at your misuse of Helen, even if expressed in her own excessive terms, justifiable in anyone's argot.

You rose to go out to them, be affectionate and vibrant, full of stories. They were, you found, innocently sleeping on their knees.

It was half past two, and the telephone began to ring. You found it to be Helen's mother, full of business even on a Sunday. She had reason to be; Helen had left quite early that morning in the station wagon, without saying where she was going. Now she'd been away for five hours and they had telephoned everyone she'd known in town. Could she possibly have called on you?

For a second you considered lying, because the question aroused a sense of your other culpabilities. All nervous reserves for facing accusers had been designated for the case of the truck-driver, and you felt it beyond you to admit to Helen's visit and the disengaged way you had let her go away.

You admitted she'd left your house about eleven that morning, and that she hadn't wanted anyone to go with her.

The mother chirruped, "But the river will be over the levee here by four. Then she'll have trouble getting just from one part of the town to another. Let alone . . ."

You felt sick. Whatever had become of sweet Helen's capable little body?

You said you'd go out immediately and look for her. But you explained that this morning's meeting hadn't been happy and that she might be parked somewhere in town, just looking at the rain, more or less.

With a sting, the mother said, "Damian, there's a flood on. Perhaps you could have swallowed your pride when there's a flood on?"

"I'll go now."

"Damian, telephone me. Please. It's a heavy wagon—one and a half tons. Surely floodwaters couldn't—"

"No." But terror for her had already dried you out. You remembered Friday night with a new immediacy, the ointment she had broken over your head that should have been saved for some king or free man.

"But ring me!" shrieked Helen's mother.

You wrote in your long untidy hand a short accusatory note to Barbara that explained where you had gone.

Four miles along, you came to the principal floodway and could see, not one-third of the way across it, the station wagon apparently firm and still on the roadbed. Water from the west moved over the swamp in a swathe perhaps five hundred feet across, sucked at the inset doorhandles of Helen's wagon, eddied about its grill at the speed of rapids. Helen sat on the roof, her hair pigtailed all over her face from hours of drenching. If she had seen you, she gave no sign.

You noticed how efficient she had been about surviving. The contour of the front windscreen was missing, so that she must have escaped by it to the engine cowling and thence onto the roof. Self-reliant, you thought, a thinker. A person with a taste in hysteria would have tried to wade the temptingly small distance to the edge of the flood and been sluiced naked and drowned.

You waved to her. She shivered, so you thought, and raised a hand towards you. When you called to her, indicating in large dumb-show gestures that you would drive to her and that she could step onto your bonnet and roof, she nodded with a broad casualness.

So you draped a burlap over the radiator and took the truck into the water; and were pleased to find it hold itself in motion. But when you had come to a stop, hard in against the rear of the wagon, the truck carriage lifted and washed sideways. In that same instant the engine stalled and you felt the rear wheels lift once more. Beyond the teeming windscreen you saw Helen on her knees, calling to you from her island, urging energy. You took a small wrench from beneath the seat and shattered the glass with it. The sudden decomposition of your frontwards vision into a wall of opaque glass cells panicked you, and you risked your hands poking holes in the granular pattern. You emerged on the bonnet, seeing the powerful water as, if anything, higher than eye-level and fabulously menacing. As steps to Helen's roof the partly opened rear windscreen and a dust deflector (of all ironic things) presented themselves, and Helen's hand was held out too.

"Well." She shivered. *"Blue Lagoon!"*

"Ah!" you squealed; for the Glover truck was sweeping round on the pivot of its front wheels and seemed about to vanish.

But "No!" you said, when it swung to the lee of the wagon until, nearly parallel to it, it faced back up the road down which you had come.

You shouted over the startling susurrus of the waters. "Your parents will have a good idea you're here, when I don't ring them back."

She nodded. "Let them get one of their friends from the Blue Water Club to lend them a powerboat."

Shifting on your hams to survey the truck, you kissed her shoulders. "Don't try to understand!" you yelled. "But Christ, I'm glad you're well!"

"Good!" she mocked you out of pink lips.

You felt some anxiety but no terror on that tiny refuge, though you prowled a little on all fours, lacking Helen's stillness; and with amazement you sensed a pleasure in her at being with you even at this price, wet and endangered and beset by moving planes of brown water that scattered the mind and bullied the memory, so that that morning's scene lost its significance.

There arose therefore a strong sentimental urge to *insist* that she marry you and form one of those penny-pinching campus unions. There seemed to be evidence, literary or otherwise, that people trapped together by rising water or stuck anchor chains had always thought compulsively of marriage. Bewildered perhaps at dusk on some Catholic Youth Club hike, and lacking a compass, your sentimental father would have rushed to suggest marriage to the lean and passively pretty girl your mother had then been.

"I think of you," you lied involuntarily, "at least a dozen times a day. I know how much I need your—you know—serenity."

She raked her hair back from her face. She threatened you. "If you marry me because I make you feel safe, I'll react. I'll have a crack-up."

You felt a sudden anger. "Do you have to be so bloody facile?"

At about four the rain stopped and steam rose from your clothes. Helen was sneezing casually; in fact, you had both become jaded by the flood that seemed to be failing to eke higher towards you. All the objective evidence that you were about to become the season's first flood casualties failed now to awe you yourself, let alone Helen.

The decisive thunderheads were marshalling, and occasionally fat drops of rain fell over your faces in handfuls. A mineral-company truck drove up to the near verge of the flood. You could see Barbara leaning from the passenger's window. Cutting a wide wake, it came up, and a sensation of unreality took you at a gulp when you saw the Frederic, whom Mr. Placer had felled last May, smiling at the wheel.

"This is Frederic," Barbara told you on dry land and without blinking.

"That's only half the news," Frederic said, not seeming to recognize his fellow drinker of all those months past. He was gay now, light, had lost the sluggish melancholy of that concussed autumn afternoon. There was a feverish confidence that he could extricate both awash vehicles, and he insisted on your help. Showing a vast willingness to endanger himself, he secured the truck and the sedan and pulled them clear, to a point where he stood furiously grinning, aggrandized to giddiness by Helen's token thanks and Barbara's abstracted concern for him.

"Tell 'em the news, then," he babbled when leaving you all at Glovers' gate.

"I will," Barbara muttered. "Later. Not now."

"No, no." Frederic was boyish. "Tell 'em now."

She focused her impenetrable eyes in her purblind yet visionary manner on some point that seemed beyond the vision of you other three. Not for the first time, you wondered if she had a cast in her eye. "Frederic and I are going to be married."

"Ah," you heard Helen say formally. "Congratulations, then, as well as thanks."

Madness now seemed unavoidable, and you found it less unlikely that they were actually mocking you than that they were planning marriage. But neither of them gave a hint: Barbara stared with astigmatic intensity; Frederick went on beaming his broad, blatant possessiveness.

You had foreseen her loss as an academic possibility, but such obscene loss was beyond all mental and emotional good sense. It was janglingly wrong for a woman who took account of every pint of milk, offcut of meat, portion of bait, to pay herself away in one lunatic spree.

"Can I see you tonight?" the dark oaf was actually asking her.

"No, not tonight. Tomorrow is a possibility."

They kissed, Barbara remotely but with a sort of devotion. So obviously obscene it was—something like pederasty—that you expected protest from Helen. But Helen was taking stock of her sodden clothes.

Nothing more was said until you were indoors, where *you* began to tremble.

"But it's foul. You can't bear his bloody vegetable children." The words themselves brought out of you a long retching bark, which both the women ignored. You sat down, grinding your brows in your hands, trying to make tears come but managing only to cough; the ridiculous unhandiness of the male when it came to express its grief! Barbara did not try comforting. Instead, you heard her speaking reasonably from the far end of the room.

"I've committed myself to him. You know the ease that people get committed to each other with. I committed myself. Or anyhow, I *was* committed. You know. You understand. It's happened to you."

Was she talking about Helen? you wondered. The accusation was ridiculous. Helen! It was as if you had forgotten she was in the room.

"You mustn't worry," Barbara went on. "You're really more of an innocent than I am. You think a person is only a matter of who he does this and that with. You think that if I was married to Frederic that's what I'd be: *Married to Frederic*. But it isn't always true. Anyhow, it wouldn't matter. These things are what the mother would call God's will. That's probably absolutely true, a better way of putting it than 'committed.'"

"You can sound reasonable," you shouted, "but you're getting revenge on me for Helen. And that's primitive as hell."

"Revenge?"

"On me. For Helen."

You became aware that Helen, still drenched, was speaking to her parents on the telephone; and when she was not speaking, the anxious yapping of Mr. and Mrs. could be heard. Looking up at the seated Helen, you saw her with her cold knees together, sobbing under reprimand.

"But I haven't got the energy to reassure you," Barbara was saying. "It's been such a day. But you oughtn't to think it's all roses for Frederic. I scare him. He's not as happy as he seems. He's only happy because he knows life's taken a sort of unavoidable turn. Because he's committed. He doesn't know what he's in for, though. He hasn't had all the schooling in that sort of thing that we have. But he was committed to asking me, and I was committed to saying yes."

"*Committed!*" you shouted. "You only know the word from the bloody news on television."

"Please," Helen said, her hand protecting the mouthpiece, "please. They think I'm in the middle of violence."

Barbara went to the veranda, where the afternoon was darkening now. Her parents' faces there were livid with the blue light of some wildlife programme on the television, but they had turned down the volume to listen to the kitchen conversation.

The mother's face was set; she claimed to have had a bad afternoon and needed to be attended to. Barbara agreed and fetched bucket and sterile rags and the proper medicines. The symptoms justified such humility.

"That young girl isn't going to stay here?" the mother asked.

"I don't know where else," said Barbara.

"The things a mother comes to," the mother uttered wanly.

"Yes," said the father as a token, staring all the time at a soundless feral contest on the screen, wild boars contesting to the death. "Yes. We'll have to start taking this condition more seriously."

Within Barbara there first rose her accustomed grey inability to speak. Numberless clichés of ripe anger, of thoroughgoing sense of misuse, were suppressed by some painful ambition that her throat would one day mould and emit an incomparable formula of revulsion.

"I'm not going on," she told them softly.

"Not any use of sulking," muttered the father, still enchanted by the boars scoring bright damage on each other with every flourish of tusks.

She said, numb at his ingenuousness, "No, I'm not going on." She referred to their suspicions that she had somehow brought on the accident. That afternoon, she said, she had experienced something that convinced her she had, even if in ignorance. And if that was so, there were surely all sorts of dangers for Damian.

"Damian!" the mother gargled, accustomed to the accident, unaccustomed to having a promiscuous son. Damian doesn't rate with me as highly as he did."

"Because of the girl?"

"It wasn't what he was brought up for."

"You've already said that," the father murmured over his shoulder, still possessed by the screen.

"You'd better start listening," Barbara told him, "and stop deceiving her." She was pleased to get that out. "She thinks it's evil for Damian to take a girl. I think it's evil for you to let her concentrate on these side issues by pretending there's—you know—somewhere in the world someone who can help her."

The mother winced between phrases as Barbara tenderly drew the foul thick milk of her disease from her udders. Wincing in this way, "Barbara," she said, "I think you must be demented if you talk like that. Or jealous."

"Jealous. Jealous?"

"That I've been chosen to bear those things." The mother gestured with a cupped hand towards her lower parts.

Barbara inhaled, not without a type of ultimate joy: suddenly, for the first time, and at last, she felt too tired for indirectness.

In this important way, her combat with Frederic, which had not been lacking in the unambiguous animality that had interested Mr. Glover on the flickering screen for the past five minutes, had liberated her.

"There's no way to get help for you. He"—she pointed to the father—"encourages you in the belief that there is, because he feels he has something to make up to you—excursions among other animals. . . ."

The father tore his eyes from the wild boars. "Barbara," he shouted, "for God's sake, that'll do. No lies." Though his pitiable urgency meant *No truth, please no truth!*

Barbara went on in sunny, clinical ruthlessness. "But you mustn't think you weren't driven to go looking for . . . other comfort."

The father was bellowing denials.

"As for me, I've done things—acts—with a man and I'm bound to him, though I don't want to be."

"You don't mean?" the father asked. He saw grandparenthood as a further comical exploitation.

"No. Nothing as obvious as a child. But we don't deserve each other, this man and me. We both deserve better and worse, in different ways."

"Thank God," the father intoned, "*you're* not educated." He meant she was devious enough, without being burdened with a knowledge of semantics.

"But the point is that you have nothing to be ashamed of. There must be millions—you know—absolute millions of people who are so full of family pride and such, so full of it all, that the only way for them to get humility is through learning they're —you know—beasts. I've learned it. About myself. And you have."

"It was bloody easier than discovering penicillin," the father admitted.

"You make me sick," the mother called out. "I am like I am because I've been chosen out. To be this."

"Chosen?" Barbara frankly doubted.

"Barbara, you talk as if there was no God."

"No, that's not the truth. Only a God is worthy to look at us and—and"—she sought for an unpretty word, one that would jolt her mother—"*pity* us," she concluded, giving in. She was reminded of a phrase she had heard somewhere: "Only a God is worthy to pity such great wounds." Or was it "tears"?

"You want to kill yourself," the father stated, with a penetration he could have shown all his life, except that blunt and patent means had always been easier to him: to dismember a calf, for instance.

"No," said the mother. "No, there's no forgiveness for suicides. Unless they're mad. And it'd be criminal in your case—with your whole life ahead of you. Besides, you can't leave us."

"I think you should come with me."

"They also serve," the mother said, "who only stand and wait."

The husband looked at his wife with a naked hatred, while between him and Barbara a palpable bond seemed to have grown, a positive discipleship. What a triumph, to lead them to freely selected deaths!

She took time to draw distinctions between the suicide which is a straight denial of life and that which was merely an escape from what was, by human standards, insufferable. The memory rose in her of Jehanne's leap from the top of the Beaurevoir tower, where she was exercising alone while John of Luxembourg's prisoner. Three kind ladies had been looking after her, Luxembourg's wife and aunt and stepdaughter, who had even offered to run up a dress for her, or show her a number of lengths of material that she would be sure to find something to her taste among. But she knew what the realities were: the bidding was running high a little to the south of Beaurevoir, where the Bastard of Wandomme, whose archer first pulled Jehanne from her horse, had been paid off by Jean de Luxembourg, who had himself been paid off by the Duke of Burgundy, who was about to be paid off by the English. Only Charles,

Jehanne's weak brother of a king, was failing to put in a tender
—he didn't want her back; he wanted the freedom of being
dominated by people of his own choosing. She knew where she
would end and disliked the prospect that there was no means
to prepare yourself against the obscenity of flame. So she
jumped. That was a sort of suicide, looked at objectively. Morally, it was escape. That was necessary to Barbara now, moral
escape. She must not end with mere concussion and a sprained
ankle, though, like Jehanne.

She said to the parents—she was swabbing her mother's tender udders now—"I want you to forgive me and die with me. I
think my father's willing. I think he's tired of the joke."

"Yeah! Yes!" said her father, catching the pitch of her gesture.
"Yeah!"

"Your condition will *not* be cured," she stated to the mother.
"Nor will mine."

"I won't take you seriously," the mother muttered. She could
gauge their sudden fire and was afraid of it.

"Yes," the father went on saying. "Yeah."

Barbara coughed and gave them the peroratory sentence. "I
want you both to forgive me and die with me."

She had three bottles of sleeping-tablets, nearly full, the result of the three inconclusive visits to general practitioners made
since she was twenty. They should all go away down the beach.
It would be wet in the open, but as you took the tablets a
wonderful warmth would suffuse you.

She asked them to promise to wait for her.

When she came inside, there was Helen seated silently at the
table, while you defended the stove corner in a permanent pos-
ture of stealth. She waited for you to take up some stance
indicating greater balance: it was hard to leave you hugging
the walls to yourself, like a mental patient. But it was no worse,
she supposed, than the demeanours and embittered minds that
some other explosive necessity—bomb or earthquake or defec-

tive electric water-heater—found members of families in every day of the sad week. In her room, on last Christmas's garlanded stationery, she remembered to compose a note for the police and any others who might tend to endow her death with an importance her life never had. She explained that her parents were ill and she didn't trust doctors, that the government wanted to convert her to bulk and she didn't want to be. It would not be such an unlikely letter—except in literacy—to get from a Campbell's Reach suicide.

Then she wrote to you, in a rush.

Beloved Damian,

If you think I have gone off because of Helen, let me assure you that I suspect Helen means little enough to you and that it was terror of me and them that forced you to attempt loving her.

I am going because of Frederic, because your mother's case is terminal, because your father wants to go. We have talked about the accident for so long. Well, I have further accidents in me. In the third drawer of my wardrobe you'll find a document in a plastic sleeve under my slips. It may have value. I think you should find out whether it has. If so, don't donate it. I know you; you'd be likely to. I think you should sell it. It would be false pride for someone as poor as you to give it away. Besides, I've been used to looking on it as a gift from one orphan to another—a peculiar kind of orphan, that is, the kind who don't lose their parents but the childhood they should have had. Anyhow, please don't just give the document away.

You have your freedom and I suppose it scares you. You'll grieve for the three of us, I know, which will interfere with your chances of being sensible even more. But let me tell you this: don't give up your freedom easily, just for the sake of a bit of animal warmth. I'm not trying to insult you, or Helen. But Helen's like me, too strong for you. Now you have the freedom to be stronger than that. You are used to being committed—pardon me, *forced* into people's orbit. Now it's all yours, to work out. No more being forced.

I love you, Damian, with every part of my body and mind. I'm surprised it doesn't show up in the surroundings and the climate, and shock my mother.

You'll always wonder—you know how you talked yesterday —how many centres all my interlocking circles of motives have. I'm sure they have many. For one thing, I hate the idea of that thin little girl sleeping with you. Never mind. It seems all the bigger circles and all the bigger centres are what they ought to be.

Don't let the police read this. Nor, if possible, the little cash book full of jottings about Jehanne.

I'd like to promise to love you past the grave—as people promise in old books. I don't know if love is recognized currency over there. So, all I can say is, to the last second of consciousness. . . . .

Barbara

Since the cash book called "Reflections on the Life" was her only outlet for melodramatic statement, she wrote in it:

I have been burned alive. Jhesus.

Her three bottles of sleeping-pills occupied a shelf in the laundry, among caulking compound and stove-cleaners. Both you and Helen had begun to speak at the table in an introspective way, eyes cast down. Once or twice Barbara and you had done that: you fictionalized yourself as you went and finished about midnight with a hollow elation and some painful hope in the future. She had been so active, arranging her departure, that she was at the door before the urge to take you against her belly by the ears and absolve you from mourning held her in the room.

"I'll be half an hour, Damian," she said. "Just cleaning up the barn a little. Then I'll make Helen and you a decent meal."

"Yes, yes," you both said, your eyes frosted with your egocentric rhetorics. "But there's no bother."

The veranda's vacancy hit her with a physical force. It seemed to have been contrived so that the ways articles were disposed implied that no one had lived here for years. The television's eye was perniciously blank; *Dairy Farming in Australia* lay under doilies in the open cupboard; the pipe lay cleaned on its side—all like exhibits in a folk museum. She was astounded by the cruelty involved in arranging objects with such swift skill and then fleeing.

She ran out into the rain, circled the house, calling softly for them, and then back to the veranda, to sniff up the positive smell of their recent presence through her rain-clogged nose.

"Where are you?" she whispered. She believed that they could be heard laughing, off in the dark, like children. She ran after them. The three small phials tucked in her pocket.

"I can't make any choice," you were explaining to Helen, "while ever I'm in *their* shadow. How could it be a balanced choice? It just couldn't be."

The clock and your stomach both told you at once that two hours had passed. Helen was wrapped in a blanket, looking very much like the flood victims in newsreels. You still wore the clothes in which Frederic had saved you.

You excused yourself and went with a storm-light to the veranda, still overcrowded with furniture and keepsakes but with the appearance of a quickly abandoned camp, and a wasteful electric light shining on it all. The barn was empty and smelled heavily of damp and an even more final desertion.

The Glover herd, you saw, shambled around the cowshed, as if the pastures were all flooded now. Going in to excuse yourself from Helen, you took ten seconds to visit Barbara's room and found, side-on in her marbled notebook, the letter for you.

You left Helen in the house and went searching. Uneasy, still she kept the fire stoked. At eleven the power went, and she and the fire were the only two poles of light in a roaring darkness, a basic darkness, the type that breeds ghosts and visions, rituals for luck or salvation, religion itself. Within half an hour she glimpsed, through a cleft in the dark, a time-embrasure whose edges glinted from firelight like quartz, a boy of perhaps ten, naked, of creamy skin, dark-haired, a little Oriental. He smiled very directly and pleasantly at her, and she saw that over his left shoulder was a white towel sodden in the centre with blood. The towel fell and the shoulder was seen to be clean of any wound. A smile of keenest gaiety came to his face.

She ran out, calling for you.

Above, the sky thundered down nasty promises against individuals and species and phenomena, and she found the huddled, frightened cattle in the yard. Catchments spewed and floodgates burst; all levees were devoured. Small's best bull was washed away, and Mrs. Glover screamed to find herself hock-deep and tripping in hard and spinning water not a quarter-mile from home. "Dad," she screamed, "Dad." Geographies were altered, the town was cut through the middle, the soil of profitable farms bundled uselessly into the bottom of Campbell's Reach or swept north on warm summer tides. Similarly bundled or swept, eons or fathoms deep, were the Glovers and their passive daughter. What futurist ploughshare would crack their bones, what sea-bottom dweller find diversion or intellectual torment in their curious remains?

In the awful tower of his freedom, Damian called out repeatedly for his remarkable sister.

More about Penguins and Pelicans

For further information about books available from
Penguin please write to Dept EP, Penguin Books Ltd,
Harmondsworth, Middlesex UB7 ODA.

In the U.S.A.: For a complete list of books available
from Penguin in the United States write to Dept DG,
Penguin Books, 299 Murray Hill Parkway, East
Rutherford, New Jersey 07073.

In Canada: For a complete list of books available from
Penguin in Canada write to Penguin Books Canada
Ltd, 2801 John Street, Markham, Ontario L3R 1B4.

In Australia: For a complete list of books available from
Penguin in Australia write to the Marketing
Department, Penguin Books Australia Ltd, P.O. Box
257, Ringwood, Victoria 3134.

In New Zealand: For a complete list of books available
from Penguin in New Zealand write to the Marketing
Department, Penguin Books (N.Z.) Ltd, P.O. Box 4019,
Auckland 10.